DATE DUE

JUDGMENT DAY

Also by Frank Roderus
in Large Print:

Charlie and the Sir
Billy Ray & the Good News
Billy Ray's Forty Days
The Wrangler

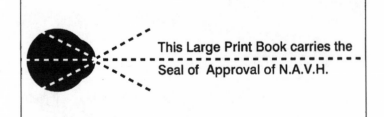

JUDGMENT DAY

Frank Roderus

Thorndike Press • Waterville, Maine

Published in 2006 by arrangement with The Berkley Publishing Group, a division of Penguin Group (USA) Inc.

Thorndike Press® Large Print Western.

The tree indicium is a trademark of Thorndike Press.

The text of this Large Print edition is unabridged.
Other aspects of the book may vary from the original edition.

Set in 16 pt. Plantin by Ramona Watson.

Printed in the United States on permanent paper.

Library of Congress Cataloging-in-Publication Data

Roderus, Frank, 1942–
    Judgment day / by Frank Roderus.
        p. cm. — (Thorndike Press large print westerns)
    ISBN 0-7862-8532-X (lg. print : hc : alk. paper)
    1. Cattle drives — Fiction. 2. Large type books.
  I. Title. II. Thorndike Press large print Western series.
PS3568.O346J83 2006
  813'.54—dc22   2006001535

JUDGMENT DAY

National Association for Visually Handicapped
------------------------- *serving the partially seeing*

As the Founder/CEO of NAVH, the only national health agency solely devoted to those who, although not totally blind, have an eye disease which could lead to serious visual impairment, I am pleased to recognize Thorndike Press* as one of the leading publishers in the large print field.

Founded in 1954 in San Francisco to prepare large print textbooks for partially seeing children, NAVH became the pioneer and standard setting agency in the preparation of large type.

Today, those publishers who meet our standards carry the prestigious "Seal of Approval" indicating high quality large print. We are delighted that Thorndike Press is one of the publishers whose titles meet these standards. We are also pleased to recognize the significant contribution Thorndike Press is making in this important and growing field.

Lorraine H. Marchi, L.H.D.
Founder/CEO
NAVH

* Thorndike Press encompasses the following imprints: Thorndike, Wheeler, Walker and Large Print Press.

Prologue

There was a dull, insistent thrumming inside his head that muted all other sounds, submerging and hiding them.

He felt fragile. A walking matchstick figure, brittle and unsteady. A shimmering, foglike haze obscured his vision and he felt oddly detached from all that was around him, as if he were outside his own body and somehow able to observe himself from above and slightly to the rear as he marched up the steps of Archer's and into the store.

He heard words, sounds that were without meaning or importance. What was important was the rack with the heavy rifles, the display case with the boxes of cartridges. He observed his own careful, deliberate actions as he took down the bear rifle. Picked up a box of ammunition. Turned and went back into the street.

He knew in a vague sort of way where he

was. Knew in a very precise and particular way where he was going. And what he had to do when he got there.

He heard a muffled, choking sound and knew quite dispassionately that it was the sound of his own sobbing.

He fumbled with the mechanism of the rifle and clawed open the box of bright, deadly cartridges.

Tears rolled down his cheeks, but he did not feel their passage on his skin. Mucus ran from his nose, across the shelf of his lip, and into his mouth. He did not taste it nor did he bother to wipe it away. It was unimportant. Everything was unimportant. Everything except what he had to do.

He moved on. Wooden. Blind to all around him.

He had . . . he knew where to go . . . knew what to do. But . . . oh, God. God!

He reached the schoolhouse steps and started up them.

1

"Whoo-eee doggies now, boys. Grab your partners and form your squares, 'cause we're gonna howl tonight."

Keenan Hemple was calling the dance, and Earl Grantham and George Marrick on a washtub bass and a concertina gave backup to Addison Truax's fiddle. Mr. Truax lost a leg at Chickamauga, but that sure didn't stop him from keeping the time with the one foot he had left.

The music started and the married folks paired off and rushed into the center of things. The single girls — not that there were so awful many of them — hung tight together underneath the hayloft, while the single boys stayed on their side of the floor on the smelly and somewhat squishy ground where normally there were horses standing in stalls. The stall walls and gates had been taken down and carried outside for the occasion, and the place had been

9

cleaned out as best could be managed. Which was pretty good, considering. But no better than just pretty good once considering was done with.

"G'wan, Johnny. Ask her," Pipper Nelson urged with a wink and a nudge.

"I'm not ready yet," Johnny Ackerman mumbled.

"Ah, by the time your nerve comes up so will the sun and everybody else will've gone home."

"Now that ain't so. I'm gonna ask her. Just you wait and see."

Across the skipping, swirling floor of gaily turned out dancers, Johnny could catch a glimpse now and then of Sarah Young, who was fifteen, soon sixteen, and just about the prettiest thing there could be short of a newborn calf or a well-set-up cutting horse.

"Promenade left and skip to m'lou," Mr. Hemple called, more or less in time to the music. Which the band was playing more or less in time to each others' instruments. "Honor your partners and back to the square."

"So where's the new schoolteacher?" Andy Wilmot wanted to know.

Johnny shrugged. The dance was being thrown to introduce the new teacher to the community, but she hadn't been on the afternoon stage. Her failure to appear hadn't been deemed sufficient reason to cancel the dance. Not after the stalls were taken apart and the place cleaned out so nice.

"I wonder will she be pretty," Pipper mused.

"Even if she is, ol' Johnny won't see. He's only got eyes for young Sarah Young." Andy batted his eyes and clasped both hands over his heart.

"You hush, Andy. You don't know nothing."

"He knows you don't have nerve enough to walk over there and ask her to dance," Pipper said.

"Well, I will. And anyway this jig is just about over."

"They're still dancing."

"Yes, but Mr. Truax has that parched and peaked look on him. He'll be taking a break pretty soon to step outside and have a nip."

"You ought to go ask can you have one with him. Maybe then you'd get nerve enough to dance with her."

"I don't know how to dance."

"Everybody knows how to dance if they really want to. You just git out there and jump around some. Nobody's gonna care what you look like."

Johnny didn't answer. He was occupied elsewhere. Just as he'd predicted, the music tailed off and quickly died once Mr. Truax stopped fiddling, and then everybody went back to lining the walls and talking. Lordy, it was loud in there. But now that the center of the floor was mostly clear, he could see across the barn to the other side without all the folks getting in his way.

Sarah was wearing a blue dress with little yellow specks on it. Little tiny flower images, he supposed those were, although he hadn't gotten close enough to see that for sure. Her hair, blond and as yellow and bright as sunlight, was done up in curls, and she had blue ribbons tied in her hair, one bow over each ear, and a blue ribbon tied tight to her neck with a little pin or doodad of some sort at the throat.

Gracious but she was pretty.

"Me and Pipper are gonna go outside and have a nip our own selves, Johnny. You coming?"

"What? Oh. Yeah. I'm coming."

He stayed where he was for a minute or two, though, yearning to walk across the floor and ask Sarah could he have the next dance. He wanted to something awful. But he knew he wouldn't, not even if he drank down Andy's whole pint of Dutch courage he wouldn't. If he tried it, he'd just get all tongue-tied and red in the face and stand there making a purantee fool of himself and the whole dang community there watching while he did it.

But he wanted to. Oh, my, but he wanted to.

After a moment more he turned his back on the crowded, noisy, hot, happy barn full of folks and went outside into the cooler night air to find the fellows and have that snort.

Lordy but that was one pretty girl in there.

2

Johnny didn't mean to get in trouble. He really didn't. It wasn't like any of this was deliberate. He was driving along slow and nice as you please, the pair of young cobs moving at a trot. That was all. A trot. A slow one at that. And here came Curtis Upshaw driving the By Jiminy wagon — it was really the BYJ but everybody called it the By Jiminy — with a pair of high-stepping browns in the harness and a gleam in his eye.

Curtis had the browns moving along at a spanking pace, in a hurry to get to town for some reason, Johnny supposed.

And Johnny's team was young and fresh and not too awful well schooled just yet, which was one of the reasons Johnny was driving them today, so they could get a little work and learn a little bit about their trade.

And Johnny hadn't put blinders on his

team today, for how could you properly school a horse to accept stuff going on around it if it didn't know there was any stuff around it?

And they were young and spooky and wanted to run anyway.

And Curtis did have that gleam in his eye.

So Johnny stepped up the pace to match Curtis. And Curtis got his browns to going a little faster. So Johnny picked it up a mite too.

And the next thing you know — he honest to Pete hadn't ever actually intended it — the two of those wagons are coming down the road side by side, just going all hell-for-leather and the horses with their ears laid flat and both Johnny and Curtis popping their whips and cussing up a fiery streak at one another and leaning forward like as if that would encourage their horses to a smidgen more speed and those old ranch wagons bouncing and rattling.

And of course there was that little curve in the road just as you got to entering town.

And Johnny was on the outside and knew Curtis had the short way onto the street, so what could he do but ease over to his right a little so as to squeeze Curtis and his browns.

Next thing he knew there was this loud thump. It didn't sound so much like a crash as a thump. And Curtis was flying off his seat and out into the road and the browns were pulling kinda sideways because one of the wheels on his rig was busted all to splinters.

"Ah, damn!"

Johnny dragged his team to a stop and jumped down and ran back fast as he could to see was Curtis broken along with the wagon. Fortunately Curtis came up laughing, and Johnny helped dust him off and the two of them sort of clung to one another, both laughing too hard to stand up straight, and then they walked over to see how bad the damage was to the By Jiminy wagon.

The good thing, well, the good thing apart from the fact that Curtis was still alive and not busted up worse than being sore for the next couple days, the good thing was that the only damage was that the right-hand back wheel of the wagon was smashed and there was a gouge the size of a small apple taken out of the bottom step onto the sidewalk in front of Mr. Perkins's barbershop.

Johnny looked up and the sidewalk wasn't empty now. Mr. Perkins had come outside to see what the ruckus was, and so had Mr. Knorr and Carl Wannsutter, who must have been inside the barbershop gossiping when they heard the crash.

"Damn you, John Ackerman, when are you going to grow up?" Mr. Perkins snapped in a none too friendly tone. "If my porch step is broken your father is going to pay for it. Just see if he doesn't."

Which was not at all fair the way Johnny saw it because it was Curtis and the By Jiminy whose rig did what little damage there was, which wasn't much to begin with, and anyhow it wasn't Mr. Perkins's step but the town's.

"Yes, sir," was all Johnny could say, though. "Sorry." Which he wasn't. He still thought the race, such as it was, had been a fine lark. He turned to Curtis and said, "C'mon. Let's haul this thing over to Mr. Tolliver and see can he put some new spokes in that wheel and maybe straighten out the tire. I'll go halvsies with you."

Curtis nodded and cut his eyes toward the sidewalk where Mr. Perkins and his fuddy-duddy customers were watching. He stood so they couldn't see, and gave Johnny a wink and a grin.

"I'll park our wagon around back of Hanson's and give him our list, then meet you at the smithy," Johnny said. He took his hat off and looked up at Mr. Perkins, who was still mad, and at Mr. Knorr and Mr. Wannsutter, who weren't, and said, "Sorry to bother you."

"I intend to tell your father about this, John," Perkins informed him.

"Yes, sir," Johnny said politely. Under his breath he added, "I'm sure you will, y' old goat."

"Did you say something, John?"

"No, sir, I was just getting a good breath. My horses got away from me, you see, and it was kinda scary. My knees are tremblin' now. But I'll be all right in a couple minutes. How about you, Curtis? Are you shaky too?"

"I am, you bet, but I'll get over it."

"Right. Now let's get that wheel fixed and tend to the things that brung us in today." Johnny bobbed his head toward the gents outside the barbershop and put his hat on and went back up the street.

He was able to wait until he got around behind the side of Hanson's ranch supply store before he busted out laughing. He hadn't had so much fun since . . . well, since last weekend at the dance and that had been five whole days now.

"I'll be right with you," he called out to Curtis as the By Jiminy rig passed by the mouth of the alley beside Hanson's, the browns carving a furrow in the dirt of the street with that busted wagon wheel.

3

Johnny drove the wagon back around to the street and down into the next block — Redhorse Butte boasted of having three business blocks, not that they were all so very full, mind you, while Conyer, over toward the north end of the basin, had only two — and parked in front of Sam Archer's general mercantile.

He knew what he wanted and where to find it, and headed straight for the huge glass apothecary jars on the candy counter, he having a serious weakness for horehound candies. His mother used to despair of ever getting his britches pockets free of the gummy residues of horehound. She seemed to consider it something of a victory when he finally learned to carry his candies in a twist of paper so the black, sticky goo wouldn't get into the cloth of everything he wore.

He stopped with one of the sweets already tucked into his cheek like a chipmunk and his hand back in the jar, stopped cold by the sound of voices from the front corner of the store. One of those sounded like . . .

Johnny began to flush with nervous pleasure just as soon as he saw who it was. Sarah was there. So were four or five of the other girls, but he paid them no mind. Sarah was there.

Today she was wearing a regular dress. Johnny wasn't sure what its original color might have been. Years of lye soap had leeched that away so now it was somewhere between a light brown and a soft gray, and might have been considered either one of those. It covered her to her throat and down her arms, but the limp and washed-thin cloth couldn't begin to conceal how slim she was — in some places anyway — or how pretty. She wasn't wearing a bonnet, which was unusual to begin with, and all the more so when Johnny saw that she had the bonnet squinched up into a wad and held in one hand, leaving her head bare and her hair agleam in the light that came in through the front window.

It was then that he saw who Sarah was talking to there. She was with Redhorse

Butte's older girls, all of them, but there was a stranger with them too standing in the center of things.

The girls were talking with a boy. Well, a man. He looked to be about Johnny's age, which was nineteen and soon twenty.

This man did not look like anything or anybody Johnny ever saw before. Not even the dry-goods drummers who came through now and then.

He was tall. A good three inches or so more than Johnny's five-foot-ten. And skinny. His frame, his face, even his fingers looked long and bony. He was blond, his hair kept longer than Johnny ever saw on a grown-up human male person, and it had a limp look about it so that it kept falling down into his eyes and he would sweep it back toward his ear with the sort of gesture a girl might make. He was clean shaven and had blue eyes and eyelashes that were near as long as a calf's and curly.

He wore light gray trousers and a dark gray suit coat and a necktie and bright yellow vest with a watch chain stretched across his belly.

And Johnny didn't like him. Not a little bit.

The fancy boy said something, and all the girls laughed. Johnny could hear Sarah's

22

laughter cut like a bell through the other noise. He always loved the sound of her laughter. Used to. Today it slipped in between his ribs like a knife going in and twisted things around in there so that for a moment he had trouble getting his breath.

"Johnny," Sarah squealed. "Come meet someone." She was smiling, but he couldn't be sure if she meant it or not, if she was pleased to see him or if she was showing off a new toy.

When he didn't step over to join them right off, Sarah came skipping down the aisle — not really skipping, that is, but she moved so light and pretty that she might as well have — and took him by the arm so she could drag him over to the clutch of young people in Mr. Archer's front corner.

"Come here, Johnny. Don't be shy. Oh, is that candy in your hand? Can I have a piece?"

He still had a fistful of horehounds as he'd been caught quite literally with his hand in the candy jar. For some reason the idea of meeting this tall SOB while he was eating candy like some little kid . . . he began to blush. Lordy, he hated that. But he knew good and well he was doing it. He could feel the heat in his cheeks and his ears and he probably was lighting up like a railroad man's lantern, and there wasn't a dang thing he could do to stop it.

Caught he was, though, and about all he could do was to open his hand and offer the horehounds around. Sarah took one and so did the other girls, except for Becky Wannsutter, who had bad teeth and tried not to open her mouth when there were people around.

The fancy boy gave the lumps of dark goo a skeptical look and refused Johnny's offer with a sneer that implied he was entirely above such childishness as candy.

"Johnny, this is Mr. Edwin Foster. Mr. Foster, this is Johnny Ackerman." She beamed up at Johnny with all the pleasure as if to indicate that she had personally invented Foster. "Mr. Foster is the new schoolmaster. He's from back East. From Pittsburgh. Isn't that exciting?"

Johnny could think of things he was more apt to be excited by, but his folks had taught him to be polite. He offered to shake hands by way of welcome.

Foster managed to be looking elsewhere at the moment, and so Johnny withdrew his hand.

Foster's attention returned and he looked Johnny slowly up and down. "You are one of those cowboys I've heard so much about?"

"I w . . ." He stopped. He still had that piece of damned old horehound in his cheek, and real quick swallowed it down so he could talk proper. "I work cows. I s'pose you could say that makes me a cowboy," Johnny conceded. He thought Foster was peering down his nose, but whether that was deliberate or just because he was taller, Johnny couldn't work out yet.

"Where are those woolly pantaloons all the newspaper and magazine drawings show?"

"They're called chaps, not panta . . . whatever. And a fella only needs woollies in the wintertime to help keep him warm. Don't need any chaps at all in the summer, not around here, 'cause there's no brush to be riding through. That's what chaps are for. T' protect your legs from brush and thorns and the like."

"Fascinating," Foster said, sounding like the information was about as boring as anything he'd ever heard. "And your pistols? Why are you not wearing pistols? I thought all you cowboys went armed with pistols and knives and such."

"I hadn't expected t' want to shoot anybody today," Johnny told him. He stopped short of adding that this state of affairs was subject to change. The truth of the matter was that Johnny did not own a revolver. For that matter, none of his friends did either. His father had one, but that was a souvenir from the war and wasn't ever taken out of the cedar chest that sat at the foot of his parents' bed.

"I see," Foster said.

"Johnny, Mr. Foster intends writing a book about the Wild West. In addition to his teaching. And wait until Sunday. Mr. Foster has agreed to join the church choir, and he has the most magnificent voice."

Sarah was a member of that choir, Johnny knew. He could always pick her voice out among the others. Sarah's singing was the best reason he knew for going to church as faithfully as he did.

"Will you be coming Saturday?" Janie Swanson asked. Janie was twelve and had a crush on Johnny, which he pretended not to notice.

"What's happening Saturday?" Johnny asked.

"Oh, dear. Did I forget to mention that? Mr. Hemple has agreed to let us use the barn again Saturday night since Mr. Foster wasn't here in time for his welcome dance.

You will come, won't you?" Sarah asked. Her dimples showed when she added, "Please come early so you can help take the stalls out again."

"I don't know. Maybe," Johnny growled.

He turned and got out of there without saying good-bye to the girls. Without paying Mr. Archer for the candies he'd taken out of the jar too. He could do that some other time, though. He wasn't in any mood to hang around in town today. Not any more he wasn't.

4

Johnny stamped his feet on the rag rug tacked down on the front stoop and stepped inside. He kicked his boots off beside the door and removed his hat, hanging it onto one of the pegs drilled into the logs close to the door frame.

"Did you remember to wash your hands, son?"

"Yes, I washed my damn hands," he snapped.

Johnny barely had time to blink before his father was standing nose to nose with him. "Boy, you apologize to your mother and you do it right now or you'll be finding you aren't too big for me to take the strop to."

Johnny stiffened. But only for a moment. He was already taller than his father and probably could whip the old man if he had to. But he didn't have to and knew he never would. Even if his father did take the razor strop to him, big as he was and considering himself a man grown, Johnny would bend over and take it. That would be the right thing to do. But he wouldn't like it. Dammit!

"Yes, sir." His father backed away half a pace, and Johnny said, "I'm sorry, Mama. I shouldn't ought to use language like that. I know better."

"All right. Now sit down. Supper is almost ready."

"Yes, ma'am."

Lewis Ackerman took his proper place at the head of the table. Johnny sat on the side, between his father and the plate his mother would get around to using once her menfolk were both eating.

"D'you remember," his father mused in a normal tone of voice, "when you were, oh, twelve or thirteen and we rode through that coulee on the north range looking for cows holding their calves in cover, and what we found instead was the last sure enough grizzly bear in this part of the country? D'you remember that, boy?"

"Yes, sir, I do."

That was the first time Johnny was allowed to ride with the grown men, and it must have been the first or maybe just the second roundup held after white ranchers started moving into the basin. Johnny trailed his pop everywhere the old man went that day, Johnny on the steady old gray gelding he'd named Bucephalus after Alexander's great war horse. The naming was a wasted effort, of course, for the horse very quickly became known as Buck. But Johnny always thought of the old horse as Bucephalus, for he was Johnny's very first steed to call his own.

Oh, he surely did remember that whole roundup, for it made him feel like he was a man to be riding along with the grownups like that.

He and his father scoured that coulee together, his pop leading and Johnny riding practically on his stirrup. They'd spooked the bear off a kill that day, one of the whitetail deer that ran in the brakes, and the grizzly stood up looking ready to fight. Johnny could still as good as see the thick slabs of muscle and the silvery gloss of the bear's fur and the wet, black, rubbery texture of its lips.

That was a scary moment, for neither his pop nor Johnny had a firearm with them. Lucky for them, the bear just stood there glaring at them with those tiny, malevolent eyes, then turned and ran away with that humpback shuffle bears have.

It ran the length of the coulee until it finally had to leave the brush and try to make a break across the open grass into the next cover beside Snyder's Creek. George Marrick had his war-surplus Spencer carbine on his saddle that day, and emptied the whole seven shots into the bear before he brought it down. George still had the cured hide laid out in his cabin like a rug, or did the last time Johnny was over there.

"I remember that bear, Pop. I surely do."

"My point, son, is that you've been acting more growly and out of sorts this afternoon than that grizzly bear was. Is there anything you want to tell me?"

"No, sir. I don't expect there's aught to tell."

"All right. Your choice. But whatever it is, you keep it out from under this roof. D'you hear me?"

"I hear you, Pop."

"I hope you do."

His mother set a plate of cornbread squares on the table along with a steaming pot of venison stew. Johnny's mother made the best cornbread in the world. He was sure of it. She always put some sugar in to sweeten it. That cornbread slathered thick with butter could be a whole meal in itself, he believed.

Stella Ackerman served her husband first, then her son, and finally she took her own place at the foot of the table.

Johnny's father grunted his satisfaction with the aromas lifting off the food that was before them. He bowed his head and clasped his hands and intoned the same grace Johnny had heard at the start of every meal since he was old enough to remember. The funny thing was that his father made the tired words sound fresh each and every time he recited them, making it clear that he meant what he said most sincerely.

"Amen," he concluded.

Johnny sighed and picked up his knife while with his other hand he was already reaching for the dish of sweet-cream butter.

His pop was right, of course. He really was feeling out of sorts this evening.

Damn that fancy boy anyhow!

5

The Ackermans didn't own a carriage, just the light farm wagon, so the first thing every Sunday morning Johnny cleaned it up and put a homemade bolster across the seat to serve as a cushion and laid a lap robe over that. The lap robe, sometimes more than one, depended on the weather, dark and heavy buffalo robes in winter, or light cotton blankets in nice weather like this when all that was wanted was to keep the dust off his mother's Sunday dress and fancy hat. His father always drove. His mother always complained about bits of dottle from his big old Sunday pipe making burn spots on the lap robe.

When he was little Johnny would sit snug between the two of them. Now that he was too big for such silliness he put a cloth down in the wagon bed and rode back there, always over on the driver's side where he could smell the tobacco smoke.

The aroma from his pop's pipe tobacco was rich and wonderful. It was one of the first scents Johnny could remember from back when he was really, really little. A couple years before, though, he'd snitched a little of it and tried smoking some in a corncob pipe Andy swiped from his father. The stuff tasted terrible. Harsh and dry and nasty. And chewing it had been worse. Johnny could still call that taste back to mind. After more than a year the taste of a chew made his stomach turn.

But he still did surely like the smell of good pipe tobacco. His father bought his by mail order, all the way out of Chicago.

Johnny put the team in harness and brought them around to hitch to the wagon, then went inside to let his parents know they were ready. His father was drinking a last cup of coffee and his mother was still fussing with the lunch basket for after services.

"All set?"

"Yes, sir."

"You brought the nose bags?"

"Yes, sir." They used to give the horses a little grain poured out on the ground where they could reach it, but some of the folks let their horses loose on hobbles during the long sermonizing and those would poach any loose grain they could get to. It resulted in some scuffles that the younger fellows found mighty entertaining. The grown folks weren't so enthusiastic about the squealing and kicking interrupting things, so the congregation passed a rule and now you had to use a bag if you wanted to grain your horses during the service. "But I didn't bring any grain. I thought we could borrow some from Mr. Johnson when we get there."

His father only laughed, knowing Johnny was joking. Adam Johnson had the reputation of being the tightest-fisted man in Montana Territory. Or maybe further afield than just this one territory. He had the habit of claiming to've forgotten to bring grain for his buggy horse and borrowing from others every Sunday. He did try to spread it around, though, so no one family was hit up for the loan week after week. It should be coming around to their turn to supply his grain again pretty soon now. Johnny couldn't think of anyone ever refusing Johnson's loan requests, always very politely phrased.

"Are you done over there, old woman?"

"Mind your own self, mister," his mother snapped back. She was smiling when she said it, though, so it was all right.

35

Johnny grabbed the picnic basket before she could think of anything more to carry, and took it out to the wagon.

"John Harold Ackerman," his mother called after him, "don't you be getting into that basket now. I know exactly how many fritters I packed and they'd better all still be there come lunchtime."

"Yes, ma'am." He wondered if she really did count them. Probably not, he decided. Besides, it wouldn't hardly be possible to ride for an hour and a half knowing his mother's famous dried apple fritters were right there in reach and him not reach in and have one.

"Mind what I said now."

"Yes, ma'am."

His folks came out, his mother setting the latch carefully so no critters pushed their way inside while they were away — not that this had ever actually happened, but she had a powerful fear that someday they would come home and find the house full of raccoons or badgers or something — and the three of them climbed onto their places. His father took up the driving lines and shook them out to get the team's attention, and they rolled out of the yard at a trot.

6

Edwin Foster's voice was every bit as easy to pick out as Sarah's. Foster's was deep and clear, Sarah's sweet and bell-like. There were seven people in the choir but so far as Johnny was concerned, Sarah and the fancy boy might as well have been standing up there singing a duet. The others might as well have been humming for all Johnny could hear them. Johnny generally liked the singing well enough. But not this morning.

He didn't much care for the way the choir was standing either. The men always stood in a row at the back with the girls up front. This morning Foster was standing immediately behind Sarah.

When they weren't singing, the choir settled down onto benches placed to the right of the pulpit, taking places in the same order as when they stood. Foster leaned forward when he was sitting. The posture brought him awfully close to the back of

Sarah's head. He seemed to be paying more attention to her than to Mr. Tolliver, who was the town's lay preacher and justice of the peace in addition to his blacksmithing.

Johnny sat through the entire forenoon service peering from Sarah to Foster and back again and being about as thoroughly miserable as any one human person could manage to make himself.

There was something about the new schoolmaster that grated on Johnny's nerves. Well, not just "something" in general. It was something in very particular and he knew it. He could see plain as day that Sarah was impressed with this fancy city fellow.

If this Foster fellow thought . . .

Johnny scowled. What Foster thought or didn't think wasn't the real problem, was it. The thing Johnny had to fret about was what Sarah Young thought.

And as best he could see right now, she was thinking mighty dang favorable about the schoolmaster.

Johnny would just have to see about that, now wouldn't he.

Somehow.

7

"Where the hell were you last night?" Pipper Nelson asked. From the gravelly sound of his voice and the pained expression he'd been wearing all morning, Johnny concluded that Pipper went on something of a Saturday night toot. Maybe a pretty good one.

"I didn't feel like going," Johnny told him.

"I never knew you to miss coming to a dance. Not when you didn't have a leg broke. And I've never known you to have a leg broke neither." Pipper reached over and took a strip of fried venison out of Johnny's hand. Johnny's mother had a way with venison. She'd strip the muscle out and slice it longways — never ever across the grain — into pieces about as thick as a thumb but longer, then dredge them in flour and fry them. There wasn't any better eating.

"Well now you can claim you've seen everything, can't you," said Johnny.

"You didn't miss much."

"You and Andy tie one on, did you?"

"We had t' do something with your share." Pipper sighed. "And maybe a little more too. Aren't you gonna ask about Sarah?"

"Nope."

"Just as well," Pipper said, then went to concentrating on the strip of tender deer meat.

Johnny knew good and well that Pipper wanted him to rise to the bait and ask what he meant by that "just as well" stuff. He wasn't going to. No, sir, he surely was not. Pipper could be just as mean as he liked. Johnny wasn't going to do it. No, sir. "Why d'you say that?" The words were out of his mouth before he knew he was going to say them. Or so he told himself.

Pipper shrugged. "She looked like she was having a pretty good time."

"She dance?"

"Yeah. Lots. Let me have another piece of your mama's deer meat, will you?"

Johnny opened his palm and held the strips out. There were three left. Pipper took two of them. Stella Ackerman's deer meat strips were famous in the whole county and there were never any left over when she brought them on Sundays.

"You should've been there," Pipper said.

Johnny shrugged and nipped a bite off the end of his last meat strip. Gracious but that was tender and nice. He finished it, then bent down and plucked a handful of grass stems to wipe the grease off with.

"Did you come on a horse this morning?" Pipper asked.

Johnny shook his head. He knew what Pipper wanted to know. Would Johnny be looking to do any racing now that dinner was over.

The little church wasn't much for size, but it was almighty busy every Sunday. First the full morning of singing and preaching, then dinner laid out on the trestle tables set on the left side of the building — the right side was reserved for the cemetery, which had five graves in it now although Redhorse Butte wasn't all that old a town — then after dinner the ladies gathered in front to chatter and gossip while the men drifted out behind the church to smoke and gossip and maybe have some races or wrestling matches. The little kids ran underfoot on all sides. Everyone took a nice long break for the social side of things, then they all went back

41

inside for another dose of hellfire and brimstone. Chores always got done late on Sunday evenings.

"I was hoping to make a match with you," Pipper said.

"What're you riding?"

"I made a swap with some Injun yesterday," Pipper said proudly. "Got me a nice-looking little paint horse, and I wanted to see how he'll run."

"Who else has a saddler you might match against?"

"Nobody who'd race with me."

"Wait until Saturday," Johnny said. "It's the end of the month. Some of the boys from the outfits farther out will be coming in town with wages in their pockets. One of them is sure to want a wager."

"Saturday's a long way off."

"Well, I'd take our team out of harness and match one of them against your Indian pony, but I think my pop would skin me if I did."

Pipper laughed.

"So who'all did she dance with?" Johnny asked, peering up at the little steeple they'd tacked on top of the church building.

"Who?"

Johnny gave his friend a dirty look.

"Couple different fellows," Pipper told him. "Luke Willis for one."

"That farm boy? I don't know what she'd see in him."

"She might've danced once . . . or twice . . . with the new schoolmaster too," Pipper said.

Johnny felt his belly lurch and come tight but he kept his face impassive.

"Where is he anyhow?" Pipper said. "He didn't leave already, did he?"

"He took his dinner with the Marricks, I noticed."

"He's boarding with them."

"I figured," Johnny said. "Last I saw of him he was around front with the women."

"He seems to have a way with the ladies, don't he?"

Johnny did not answer that. The problem was that it was true. Sarah hadn't hardly been able to keep her eyes off him all through dinner. "You didn't bring a bottle in your saddlebags, did you?"

"Damn, Johnny, not to church!" Pipper grinned. "Besides, I already drank everything I could get my hands on. I'm telling you, buddy, you should've been there last night."

"I'm just as glad I wasn't."

"What's happening over there?" Pipper

asked. He was looking at a clutch of men and boys who were standing well away from the back of the church.

"I dunno but let's go find out." Whatever was going on, he figured, it was likely something that would take his mind off his concerns. And that would surely be welcome. The two friends hurried along to join the others.

8

"A *foot* race? You're kidding, right?"

"Why not?" Elmer Ayres said. Elmer worked for the Rocker T. He was a nice fellow, a little older than Johnny and his friends. Elmer came from Texas and made no bones about the fact that he would be going back there once winter came. "We don't have the horses for any good match races." He grinned. "And I don't want to set another couple hours on those benches without getting loosened up somehow. So why not a footrace."

"Count me in."

"Me too."

"Me three."

Johnny shrugged. "Sure, why not." He hadn't raced anybody on his own feet since . . . well, probably since they moved to this country and took up the land for raising cattle, and Johnny was just a

45

button when they moved up here from Kansas.

"May I run too?"

Johnny's head snapped around in response to that voice. It was the schoolmaster surer than hell. Johnny hadn't noticed him join the bunch, but there he was, hair falling down in his eyes, smug look on his ugly face, acting like he was some-dang-body. Johnny glared at him, but Foster didn't seem to notice.

"Sure, you bet," Pipper said. Pipper, dang it, who should have known better than to give this Edwin Foster fellow the time of day but didn't have sense enough to know that.

"Are there stakes to be wagered?" Foster asked.

"We, uh, well gener'ly we race horses. But, well, yeah. Gener'ly whoever runs puts up a little stake. Not much, mind. It belongs to the winner."

"And what about the second-place finisher?" Foster asked.

"Close only counts in horseshoes," Johnny said, his voice coming out kind of low and nasty. "Losers don't get nothing."

"Fair enough," the schoolmaster said, still smiling that same smug smile.

"Everybody who wants to run put up a

dime to enter," Earl Grantham said, taking charge. That was all right. Earl was too old to be in the race himself, although he sometimes would get caught up in things and ride in the horse racing. "I'll hold the stakes and pay the winner at the end. The course will be to run back into town, make a turn around Perkins's outhouse, then back to the start-finish line. Which will be" — he used the heel of his shoe to drag a line in the dirt — "right here. Is everybody clear about that?"

"Which one of those is Perkins's?" the schoolmaster asked.

Mr. Grantham pointed it out. "Clear now?"

"Yes, thank you."

"All right, boys. Everybody ante up. Ten cents each."

"Will you take an I.O.U.?" Pipper asked. "I only had a nickel left after, uh . . . I only had a nickel to my name this morning and I already put it in the collection basket."

"Markers will be accepted," Grantham ruled. That brought a few grumbles and a few more murmurs of approval.

Johnny fished around in his pocket. He found a quarter there. "Here. I'll pay for myself and for Pipper too."

Mr. Grantham dropped the quarter into his coat pocket.

"I'd take my nickel in change if you don't mind," Johnny reminded him.

Grantham laughed. "I just thought you were being generous."

"Not that it really matters," Johnny said. "I figure to be the one taking the pot anyhow." That was pure bravado. He couldn't run worth a lick and he knew it. But then all he cared about was getting back to the line ahead of the schoolmaster anyhow.

Over to one side Foster was jumping up and down and swinging his arms in windmill circles. Johnny thought he looked like a locoed prairie chicken.

Johnny shucked his coat and necktie, tugged his hat down snug, and figured he was ready. Most of the other fellows were doing pretty much the same. Not Foster. He had to be different. He took off his coat and his tie, but shed his vest and shirt as well. Johnny had thought the fellow looked soft. He wasn't. He was lean and fit. It just could be that he could run.

Johnny took another look and noticed the schoolmaster's lightweight shoes. Johnny and most of the rest of the fellows were wearing their boots, which were perfect for riding but not so grand for walking, and they were heavy as well. On an impulse — for he did *not* intend to come in second — Johnny kicked his boots off and stripped his socks off as well, dropping them into the boots for safekeeping. No point in tearing them up by running around outdoors in them. His mama had enough trouble keeping up with the holes he wore in his socks without that.

"Is everyone ready?" Grantham called out. "Come to the line, please. Does anyone have a pistol I can use for the starting signal?" No one did. "All right then, listen close. I'll have to call it out. On three now, boys. One . . . two . . . *three!*"

9

"Is that better, dear?"

"Yes, ma'am." He wasn't at all sure that this was true, but his mother wanted it to be so and therefore he would tell her that it was. He couldn't help wincing, though, when she dipped her fingers into the lard can and applied more of the stuff to his bruised and battered feet.

"Did I hur—"

"It's all right, Mama. Honest." What else could he say. The whole truth was something else again.

He had expected the gravel and sharp stubble and all that. What he'd forgotten about was all those low-lying little cactuses that lay hidden in the grass. Running barefoot had chopped the bottoms of his feet as if he'd been running over flint and broken glass so that he'd ended up limping in in dead last place, bleeding and hurting and angry with himself for not thinking.

His folks put him into the back of the wagon and drove home without even waiting for the evening preaching.

Worse yet, his mother had spent a good hour and a half using tweezers to pluck out as many cactus spines as she could find by lamplight. Come daylight she probably would have to do it again. And in the meantime he wouldn't be able to do his share of the choring so that his father's work would be affected too.

He'd gone and made kind of a mess actually.

"Hold still, dear, while I wrap them with clean linen. That will keep the dirt out and the grease on."

"Yes, ma'am."

And to make it all the worse, that blasted schoolmaster trotted home at the head of the pack, leading everybody else by more than a rod, for crying out loud. And hadn't all the girls been cheering and happy about that!

It wouldn't have surprised Johnny if his father'd been so mad he busted a doubletree over Johnny's back. But all either of his folks did was cluck with worry and tut-tut some while they brought the wagon around and loaded him into it, by which point his ears were burning and his

51

feelings were hurting more than his dang feet did.

The whole dang community was there to see it all. Including Sarah. Including that fancy boy schoolteacher. Including just every-dang-body.

"Hurt?" Not but every least bit of him, that's all that hurt.

"No, ma'am, it's fine. Really."

"There. Now hold still. You can't climb that ladder to the loft, son. I'll carry your mattress down and lay it out on the floor like a pallet. You can sleep there until you are up and around again."

"I didn't mean to be such a bother, Mama."

"Shh. I know. Now lie still while I finish this last wrapping."

If he weren't too old to cry he'd bawl his head off right about now, Johnny thought. Heck, he felt enough like it as it was. But that wouldn't do at all. Even though he surely did feel like it. And that was the truth.

10

Johnny was uncomfortably aware of his father's big — and filthy — chore boots flopping around underneath him like some new kind of snowshoes. The thing was, he couldn't get his own boots on, not with his feet having to still be greased and wrapped, so the best he could do was to wear his pop's old castoffs.

There was no way, though, he was going to miss going out on the gather. Rounding up the cows, late spring and early fall, was a real occasion, when all the men and the near-grown boys got together.

Being out there, everybody working together, talking and visiting and neighboring, was almost as important to them as the business side of getting the herds put together and culled. They'd sell off whatever they wouldn't be able to carry through the winter, and make sure the rest were grazing close in where they could be kept an eye on through the hard months. And Lordy, Montana did have some hard months.

Anyway, he was going. If he had to ride barefoot he'd have wanted to go. This way he could protect his feet and still do a day's work along with the other fellows.

As for taking care of the greasing and wrapping along the way, well, his mama didn't have to know it, but Johnny just figured to keep these floppy old boots on the whole time they were out. It wouldn't be but three, four, maybe five days. Or so. That wasn't so much. Besides, Johnny didn't think he could do the wrapping part of it. And he surefire was not going to let himself be seen asking his pop or anybody else to doctor on him.

He clomped and stumbled his way out to the corral and took a rope down off a post, let himself inside, and sorted the rope into a loop and loose coils.

His pop wanted to start off on the old gray horse that he'd had about as long as Johnny could remember. The gray was too old to really do any work, but it didn't know that. His father would use it to get out to the far camp where they would start the gather, then he would switch to others while they were making the circles and pulling the critters together.

Johnny didn't really need to throw a loop to catch the gray. It was so tame it would come to hand if a body had a bit of fruit or piece of bread to offer. Even so, he eased around in the bunch of horses until he found a good spot and tossed a loop across the backs of some of the others to catch the gray, which whinnied and threw its head like it was highly offended. His father had warned him to do it that way. Said something about giving the old horse its dignity among the others. Johnny wasn't entirely sure about that, but he did it the way his pop wanted it done.

Once it was caught, that or any other way, the gray was agreeable. Johnny threw his pop's gear onto it, draped the headstall over the saddle horn for safekeeping, and took the horse outside the corral to stand tied to the top fence rail.

Back inside the corral Johnny looked the bunch over — not that there were so very many to choose from, the Ackermans' Rafter A not being a particularly big outfit — and decided on a leggy brown animal for himself. The brown was rangy and scarred and kind of ugly to look at, but it had an easy gait. More to the point, the horse lacked cow sense and could be better used getting to and from than going out and working.

He put enough horses in between himself and the brown that the homely thing wouldn't know which he was after, made a smaller than usual loop, and sent it hard and fast at the brown's head. The horse ducked, but too slow, and the loop got down past its muzzle to cinch up snug around its neck.

"Gotcha," Johnny chortled.

There was a flurry of stamping and squealing as the other horses scattered out of the way like a covey of quail coming out of the grass.

Johnny braced himself — that hurt a little, putting strain on his feet like he had to do, but he didn't have time to fret about that at the moment — and played the brown like a trout on a string until the horse decided it couldn't get loose and so might as well give in and pretend to be docile.

Once he was sure the brown was done with its tomfoolery, he took it outside the corral and got it saddled and tied alongside the gray.

Inside the house his pop would be having a last cup of coffee, and his mother would be clucking and fussing over the bag of treats she'd been putting things into, changing her mind and taking things out to replace them with something else for the past four days. All the outfits in the drainage pitched in to provide a store of foods that they would carry on a wagon along with all the bedrolls and medicines and tools and such, but all the wives always put up pokes of extras for their own men's special tastes.

Johnny wondered if the women knew how those bags of goodies got compared and passed around once the first camp was made. By the second or third day all that stuff would be used up and gone, shared out to the young ones.

What the men shared in the evenings was the liquor. They pitched in together in common for that too lest some of the more hard-nosed women object and somebody be left without any.

Last year his pop had told Johnny he was too young to have a drink with the grownups.

Not this year. Johnny figured he was plenty old enough now.

He stuck his head inside to tell his pop they were ready to go and better get a move on if they expected to reach the others before the break of day. Never mind that day had already broken, the sun by now halfway up from the horizon.

His father laughed and winked and gave his mom a big hug, then Johnny had to endure one too and a wet kiss on the cheek as well, as if he was still a little kid or something.

His father loaded Johnny with the bedrolls and the goodies bag. Everything else had already been carried over to the I Bar to be put onto the wagon as they were the one supplying it this time.

"Old woman," his father said in a mock stern voice, "don't take in any handsome boarders while we're away. We don't figure to be gone that long."

"Get out of here, both of you," she shot back at him. "You're getting underfoot."

His father growled something that Johnny couldn't hear, then turned away toward the door.

"Lewis."

"Yes?"

"You take care, you hear? Take care of both of you."

His pop nodded, serious now, and went back to give her another kiss. Then he smiled and said, "Come on, son. We've work to do."

Johnny felt pretty good when they went out to get a start in the cool of the morning.

11

They drove the Rafter A's band of horses into the bunch with all the others, and Johnny waved to young Benny Knorr, who was making his first gather and wasn't much bigger than the hat he had pulled down low over his eyes. Johnny would've bet he had half a bedsheet folded and stuffed into the band of that old hat to make it fit.

The youngest ones were always given the job of tending the remuda. It was easy work for them to do and let them be of serious use. The problem, of course, was that everyone had to catch out his own mount for the day since the young boys generally weren't good enough with catch ropes or horse sense to go into the herd and rope out the exact mount each rider might want. Johnny didn't mind that, but some of the older men grumbled about it.

"Hey, Benny," Johnny said as he turned

the horses over to him. There was another youngster riding on the opposite side of the remuda, but Johnny couldn't see who it was through all the dust raised by the horses' hoofs.

Benny sat up tall in the saddle and gave Johnny a nod, just as solemn and serious as a boy could get. But then he was out here working and didn't have time for frivolity.

Johnny's father was already over by the fire where there was coffee boiling and gossip flowing. Once the Rafter A bunch was in with the others, Johnny rode by the wagon to toss his bedroll in with all the others, then dismounted and tied his horse to the tailgate next to half-a-dozen others.

Pipper and Andy and some of the other fellows were standing together off away from the grown men who were at the fire. Johnny ambled over that way to join them.

He was almost to them, too close to turn and skeedaddle without being noticed, when he saw who was with them.

"Hi, Johnny. Say, you already know the schoolmaster, don't you?" Andy said, his expression innocent. It was pretty obvious that Andy was not aware of how Johnny felt about this interloper.

Foster stood and smiled and extended his hand. He was acting much friendlier now than he had that day at the store just after he arrived. He looked about as excited as little Benny Knorr.

"You know Ed is interested in the West," Andy nattered on. "So I told him he oughta come see what a proper roundup is like."

"I'd of thought you'd be busy at the school now," Johnny said, trying not to sound as surly as he felt.

"We won't begin the next term until Monday," the schoolteacher said. "I promised to be back in time for Sunday services . . . I have to sing in a duet then, you see . . . but that gives me time enough to ride the range with you chaps until Saturday."

"Uh-huh." With any kind of luck, Johnny figured, that would be time enough for Foster to get in a storm and bust his damn head open. Or something.

"You have no objection, I trust?" Foster said.

"No. Of course not." Objection? Hell, yes, he had an objection. Lots of them, in fact. But not the sort he could come right out and talk about.

"I really do appreciate this opportunity. I've read so much about the process of gathering bovines. I never expected to see it for myself."

Johnny grunted. Bovines. Johnny'd never heard them called that in his life until now. The dang schoolteacher couldn't call them beeves or cows or cattle like any ordinary human person. No, they were bovines. The fellow was disgusting, that was all. Just plain disgusting.

"Andrew was good enough to take me under wing," Foster went on. "Apparently there is quite a lot to learn."

"Oh, it ain't all that much," Johnny said. "Could be you'd want to ride with me some too. Let me teach you a few tricks." He could think of several things in particular he'd like to teach this stuffy schoolmarm in long pants. Yes, sir, he could think of quite a few tricks to teach him.

"You are very kind," Foster said with a broad smile. Johnny had the oddest feeling, something to do with the way Foster's eyes gleamed maybe, that the schoolteacher was less than sincere when he said that. Like as if Foster really did know the truth about how Johnny felt toward him.

"Yeah, well, we'll see about that later, right?"

"As you wish," Foster said.

Dang fellow wouldn't look so smug stretched out on the ground with his face in the dirt, Johnny thought.

The schoolmaster shook his head and murmured, "Look here now. Not a single pair of those pantaloons . . . was it chaps that you called them? . . . and not a single firearm in sight. Amazing."

"Yeah, and sometimes you'd think we was damn near human," Johnny said. "O' course you'd be wrong to think that." He turned and left his friends, going instead to join the older men at the fire.

12

"Let's get around, boys. We've miles to cover," Mr. Becker hollered. Ira Becker and his I Bar supplied the wagon for this fall working, and that made Mr. Becker the wagon boss, so to speak. Any really major decisions, not that there were apt to be any, would be discussed among all the owners, but for the day-to-day stuff Mr. Becker took the lead. Like he was doing now.

The way they would do this, they would travel straight out as far as the drainage ran, all the way out to the string of low hills where the cows liked to graze in the relative cool there during the summer months, then start putting everything they found into a single herd.

They would drift slowly back, adding any cows they could pick up along the way, until all the animals were together.

Once they were closer to town they would sort them in separate bunches. The long yearlings that could be sold as feeders or the culls that weren't needed for breeding or the fat steers left over from being missed or deliberately kept over from previous gathers, those would be held apart to be driven down to the river to where there were buyers waiting. The breeding stock or potential bulls and whatever young steers the men thought they could feed over the winter would be scattered on the grass close around Redhorse Butte.

These carryovers would be expected to make their own living on the stem-cured prairie grasses, but they were held as close as possible so they could be reached if need be. Come the hard freezes and deep snows, the men would have to chop ice to keep water holes open for them. Or chop down cottonwoods in the bottoms so the cows could eat the bark. In winter a man's best tool wasn't a rope or a branding iron but a sharp ax.

All that was yet to come, though. For now the coffee cups were shaken out and stuffed into saddlebags. Pipes were lighted. Bladders emptied. All the little last-moment things. Then everyone pulled his cinches snug and climbed into the saddle.

"Everybody ready? Let's get to moving,"

Mr. Becker sang out from the back of the wagon. Then he stepped from it onto his saddle and led the way.

There was a sense of excitement in the air, what with so many men and horses all together, and Johnny was enjoying himself in spite of the schoolteacher being included.

That was until he saw what that damn Foster was riding.

"Psst! Pipper. C'mere."

Pipper reined his horse closer and Johnny jerked his head to the side, leading his friend a few yards out to the side of the crowd.

"That horse the fancy boy is riding . . ." Johnny began.

Pipper grinned. "Uh-huh. It's the one you think it is. Tell you something else too. He brought along a string o' four mounts, God knows why, except I suppose he figured he shouldn't ought to play favorites. Pretty much every girl in town wanted him to take the borrow of her pet horse once they heard he was coming with us. I heard Mr. Marrick say he's never seen so much company in one parlor without anybody being dead as when the ladies flocked to call on Mr. Foster."

"Mister? What the hell for are you

calling him 'mister'? He's not any older than us."

"Aw, you know. He's the schoolmaster. What should I call him?"

"I could think of a few things," Johnny said.

"I swear, John, you look mean as a rattlesnake when you say that. Calm down, will you? Foster is the first new an' interesting person to come to this town in . . . hell, since there *was* a town here. That's all it is. He's different." Pipper laughed. "And he don't smell like horses. Didn't until now anyway. Time he gets back he'll smell of wood smoke and horse sweat just like the rest of us. Maybe that'll take some of the bloom off that bush."

"I don't like the son of a bitch riding Sarah's horse," Johnny said, stubbornly returning to the original point of his anger.

"You want me to drop a loop over him an' drag him off it?" Pipper asked.

"You're making fun of me," Johnny snapped.

"Now I just asked you a question, that's all."

"Do I want him dragged, I won't pass the pleasure along to you. I'll damn sure do it myself."

"Jesus, Johnny, I wish you didn't sound so serious when you say that."

Johnny scowled. Then shook his shoulders as if trying to physically shake off his mood. His strained features relaxed a little, and he said, "Sorry. I ought to set back and enjoy myself. It's too fine a day to fret about anything."

"That's the spirit, buddy," Pipper said with a grin. "We got the world by the tail here. No sense in letting anything spoil it." Pipper waved a pointing finger toward the broad, open sweep of the horizon — the huge sky, rolling grass, dark slashes of trees and brush to mark the coulees and the distant bulk of the hills off to the west. "It's grand, ain't it?"

"I expect that it is at that," Johnny agreed.

But he still resented the schoolteacher being given Sarah's pet ladyhorse to ride.

13

They nooned along Rodgers Creek. Since they needed to make miles on this first day, with no cows to slow them down, they built only a small fire and boiled coffee, but ate cold out of a bag of biscuits Mr. Becker supplied and dipped the biscuits in a pan of molasses. They did that every year, and every year Johnny grumbled about it. The dang molasses didn't taste anywhere near as good as it sounded.

He got the impression that Foster didn't much care for it either. The schoolteacher made a sour face after he took the first bite and didn't go back for seconds.

"They say," Johnny said in a loud enough voice that he was sure the schoolmaster would hear, "that Indians use a heap of molasses." Johnny and all the rest of the younger ones were gathered in one bunch hunkered down close by the fire while the grown men, Lewis Ackerman included, sat on a clutch of felled logs left over from where snowed-in cows had once been fed.

"They like the taste?" Andy asked even though he probably knew good and well what Johnny intended leading up to here.

"No, it ain't the taste so much. Though it's true they do like to eat anything that's sweet. No, sir, what the Indians use molasses for is torment."

"Torment. What d'you mean by that?"

"I mean you don't never want to be caught out alone by any band of Indians. They're mostly peaceable these days, but you know as good as I do that a white man alone is still fair game for their devilishness."

"Sure I know that they'd take a scalp if they thought they could get away with it," Elmer Ayres said. "We all know to be careful about that. But what does molasses have to do with it?"

"You don't know neither?" Johnny shook his head and directed his attention to Elmer. But out of the corner of his eye he could see that Ed Foster was paying close attention. "If you get caught by one of those devil Sioux . . . they're the worst, you know, though the Cheyenne and the Arapaho are near as bad . . . what was I saying? Oh. Right. If you get caught by the Sioux, what they'll do if they think they have time is to strip a man naked and stake him out on the ground flat on his back and all sprawled out with his arms and legs held wide apart." Johnny took another bite of the molasses-soaked biscuit.

"You still haven't said what molasses has to do with anything," Elmer complained.

Johnny was beginning to think that Elmer wasn't playing along, that he really didn't know. "Well, see, after they get you staked down so you can't move hardly a muscle, they pour molasses all over you. And I do mean *all* over you."

"I wouldn't like that," Elmer said. "It'd be awful hard to wash off."

"Washing isn't something you'd have to worry about, Elmer. Not never again."

"How come?"

" 'Cause what that molasses does, it draws ants. Biting ants. You ever been bit by an ant? Burns like a hot coal on your skin, don't it."

Elmer nodded.

"Exactly. Which is what the Indians want for to happen. They put the molasses on to draw ants onto you, and next thing you know there's ants all over you. In your nose and into your ears and crawling in the

71

corners of your eyes. They sting an' sting. You'll scream till your throat breaks, but all them Indians will do is think it's funny. Just about the funniest thing they ever did see. They say the Sioux in particular love to hear a white man beg to be shot or whacked with an ax to be put out of their misery, but the dang Indians won't lift a hand to kill him, for that would be merciful and there's no a drop of mercy in any one of them."

"The way I hear," Pipper put in, "a man goes plumb out of his mind once the ants get to him. They'll kill him eventually, but his mind goes a long while before that ever happens. It just hurts him so terrible bad that he can't help it. He loses his mind and he's still screaming when he finally dies and ends it."

"Are there Sioux around here?" Ed Foster asked.

"Sure. There's a reservation full of them just down that way a couple days' ride," Johnny said, hooking a thumb toward the southeast.

"Those reservation Indians are peaceful now, are they not?" the schoolmaster asked.

"Peaceful as lambs," Andy said. "As long as you outnumber them."

"Or there's army soldiers close by," Pipper added.

Johnny said, "It hasn't been all that long ago that they first whipped General Crook and then ate up ol' Custer for dessert, you know. Just a few years. But that devil Sitting Bull is still up there in Canada, wild and free as he ever was. And they say he wants to bring his band and come back down here."

"Besides, they all of them think of the reservation is a place to hole up in winter and draw those free government rations. A lot of them will come through here in summertime, going over to the hills to hunt."

"Sometimes it's cattle they're hunting."

"Sometimes it's white men. That's what I've heard."

The discussion was general now, everyone pitching in with a fact or a rumor.

Now that he'd gotten the thing started, Johnny settled back and watched Ed Foster's eyes get bigger and his scrawny shoulders kind of hunch in on each other as he tried to look around behind him without anybody noticing.

Johnny surprised himself. He was enjoying this nooning in spite of the dang molasses.

14

Now that they'd been in the basin long enough to get some history behind them, things were pretty comfortable. Come fall, they always came out to the same place for the starting camp, just like every spring they went to the same place miles southeast from town to start the after-winter gather, the cows generally drifting south over the winter no matter how hard they tried to keep the fool creatures close to home.

By now those camps were becoming fairly comfortable, with more or less permanent, stone-built fire pits and even some split logs set up as benches. It was nice, especially considering that each starting point was only used one night each year. But then it was the youngsters who did all the actual work involved, under the direction of the grown men.

This year it tickled Johnny that he was one of the ones seated on a bench directing the labor of the younger ones as they brought in wood to cook with and plenty more for a roaring huge fire for the evening.

Not that the young ones paid any mind to him, not with a couple dozen other older men who were also giving them helpful advice. They didn't pay Johnny any more mind than he'd ever paid to the grownups when he'd been bringing wood in those several years past.

It was getting harder to find good firewood by now. All the blowdowns had been gathered up and dragged in during previous fall roundups. Johnny knew because always before he'd been one of the boys out with horse and rope, snagging chunks as big as he could manage and skidding them into camp.

This year the lucky little peckerwoods had it easy to start with, though. There was some wood left over from last fall's gather, and they were able to get the cooking fire started first thing when they unsaddled and got their gear laid out.

Johnny lined up at the wagon like the rest to find his bedroll and spread it. He wasn't delighted to see that the schoolmaster put his blankets — he didn't have a proper canvas bed, just a wad of blankets rolled up and tied tight with twine — over beside Andy Wilmot's. But then Andy had kinda taken Foster under his wing, God knows why.

While the young ones brought wood in, the men sat nipping at a little whiskey to fortify themselves against the cold of the coming night, and the older men talked. Easy talk, low and pleasant, about cows and grass and weather.

Later on, once it came dark and the bunch of them were surrounded by a huge halo of dancing firelight, Tom Knorr fetched his guitar out of the wagon and began to play. They got to singing, just a few voices at first, but soon everybody pitching in. Then the rest hushed and sat there just listening when the Texas cowboy Elmer Ayres got to singing "Faithful Pony Little Red."

Elmer had him a heckuva voice. It could make you as good as see things happening, and Johnny wouldn't have admitted it for the world but by the end of that song, when Little Red's heart burst and he gave his life for that of his owner, Johnny's eyes were stinging and wet. It was just a good thing it was dark and no one else could see.

Johnny turned in soon after that, going

off by himself to find his bed and crawl in.

The fellows were still singing so that the last thing he heard was Elmer's voice coming soft to him in the night.

15

Johnny hauled the horse's head around close to his stirrup and stepped into the saddle. He knew pretty well what to expect.

The brown horse with the jagged scar on its nigh shoulder was a jumper, but it was an honest enough horse. It'd give a fellow about all he wanted, but it never cheated. Never threw itself over backward to crush him nor sideward to unseat him — which Johnny always found harder to ride than just about anything else — but went hard and heavy at straight-out bucking.

The saddle leather was hard and cold in the morning chill, and for the first few jumps he wasn't altogether sure he was going to stay on top of the brown long enough to get the seat warm.

He jammed his father's oversized and floppy boots deep into the stirrups, mindful of the fact that he'd damn well better ride the critter down once he did that lest he be dragged back to the corral. And the home place corral was, what, thirty miles away or better. Then about all he could do was hang on tight as a tick on a hound's ear.

The brown carried him high and came down with all four legs stiff, jarring him so hard it was a wonder he wasn't peeping over his own belt buckle, his spine was surely pounded down that short.

A couple more of those and he could feel the blood commence to leak out of his nose. He sniffed it back to keep it from running down onto his shirt and hung tight.

It wasn't so bad, though. He could feel the brown horse's strength wane and could hear the breath huffing and wheezing through those wide-flared nostrils.

Soon as he knew he had the brown whipped, he leaned back and raked its shoulders with his rowels a couple times to remind it who was gonna be the boss today. Otherwise there was a chance the horse might want to try him again the next time Johnny stepped off. And the truth was that he didn't want to go through this morning ritual any more than the brown probably did.

A couple more halfhearted jumps and he

reined the horse in a hard wheel to the left, then back around to the right, then stopped and let the both of them have a breather. Once he got to that point, it was safe enough to let his reins hang slack. He loosened up and hooked a knee over his saddle horn so he could relax while he looked at whatever else there might be to see in the half-light of breaking day.

Over on the far side of the remuda he caught Andy's eye and gave his friend a brief, barely noticeable shake of his head.

Andy looked like he wanted to protest, but Johnny gave him a hard look, and Andy let be.

Young wrangler Ben was just then bringing a smallish roan horse out of the bunch and leading it over to the school-teacher.

Damn Foster apparently didn't even know how to throw a saddle onto a horse's back, for Johnny could see him saying something to the boy — who after all would be one of Foster's pupils come the end of this gather — and Ben, who was half the schoolteacher's size, took care of blanket, saddle, and bridle for him.

The stirrups were already set to the right length after yesterday's riding. Ben wrapped his hand tight around Foster's borrowed bit even though it wasn't really cold enough yet that a body had to worry about warming it before sticking it into a horse's mouth. Perhaps because the boy went to that trouble, the roan accepted bit and bridle without a fuss. Which Johnny had been hoping for but was far from being certain about.

Johnny was really proud of the kid. Ben kept a completely straight face when he handed the reins over to Ed Foster, then took hold of the roan's cheek piece while the schoolmaster crawled awkwardly aboard and tried to get both himself and his reins sorted out.

The youngster played it fair as fair could be. He let Foster get himself set nice and solid on the saddle and his feet snug in the stirrups before he let go of the headstall and got the hell out of the roan horse's way.

The roan bogged its head and set its feet and then just sort of exploded in all directions at once, squealing and stomping so hard it wouldn't have been surprising if fire and smoke started coming out of its nostrils.

Johnny was grinning.

It was a positive amazement, he thought, not for the first time, just how very much alike Mr. Wansutter's roan cutting horse and his daughter Becky's tame little ladyhorse looked, although of course both of them came from the same sire and dam.

Yessir, that was the sort of mistake anybody could make, especially a young and inexperienced boy working in such poor light. Yessir, anybody.

Johnny winked at Ben, who was laughing right along with him. And for that matter, right along with pretty much everybody else in the outfit, for the schoolmaster and the little roan had become the primary object of attention for everyone present.

Indeed, there was one helluva grand show in progress.

For just about, oh, three or maybe four seconds. Then Johnny put the spurs to his brown and set off to run down and recapture Mr. Wansutter's runaway roan. He'd let someone else gather up whatever was left of the schoolteacher.

This roundup wasn't starting off too awful bad, he decided.

16

By the time Johnny got back with the roan, Mr. Becker and Ben's dad Tom Knorr were giving poor Benny what-for.

"If you don't have any better sense than that, boy, this will be your last roundup for a long time. You won't be back out here until you're grown enough to know the difference between a mare and a gelding, I can tell you that," Mr. Knorr said in a voice that wasn't loud but sure was disgusted.

Young Ben swallowed hard, and Johnny thought he could see tears gathering shiny but unshed in the corners of his eyes, but he kept his head up and his mouth closed.

"We depended on you, Benny," Mr. Becker put in. "That young man could have been seriously hurt. Really serious. He could have broken a bone. Or even worse. Then how would you feel?"

Johnny glanced over toward the fire,

where everybody was gathered around Ed Foster, hovering over him like he was a sick calf instead of just some fancy boy that had no business being out here to begin with. The schoolmaster didn't look particularly hurt. A little dusty and rumpled maybe, but that was all.

"What do you have to say for yourself, son?" Tom Knorr demanded.

Ben looked at his dad with big, sad eyes, but he didn't say anything. Johnny knew how he must be feeling. Going on a roundup was something special. It was something grown up. Now it looked like Ben's first might be his last for a while.

But the boy didn't make any excuses or offer any explanations. That seemed mighty admirable. Especially under the circumstances.

Johnny stepped down off his brown and handed the reins of Mr. Wansutter's roan gelding to Benny.

"Ben doesn't want to point fingers at anybody," Johnny told the gentlemen, "but the truth is that I'm the one made the mistake this morning. I was right there getting my horse and I saw Ben was making a loop, so I asked him which he wanted, for I already had a loop built ready to throw. He said I should rope out Becky's roan mare.

"Mind now, it wasn't hardly light yet, and I was looking over top of the horses' backs, not down underneath them. Which I suppose I should have done once I had hold of the roan, but I didn't.

"Anyway, now I can see how different the two of them are. The mare has a snip and one white foot. This cranky little sonuvabitch has more white on his face and none on his feet. I can see that now, but I never paid no mind earlier.

"Point is, gents, it's my fault the schoolteacher got in a storm this morning. My fault alone. I want you both should know that." Johnny reached over and gave Ben's shoulder a reassuring squeeze.

"Is that the truth, son? Did Johnny bring out the gelding instead of the mare? Tell me honest now. Did he?"

"Yes, sir," Benny said. "That's the truth. Johnny offered to rope the gelding out of the herd for me."

And so he had. Ben wasn't lying.

Ira Becker grunted and gave Johnny an evil look. "You're saying it was an honest mistake? Is that what you're saying, John Ackerman?"

Johnny only shrugged. Which was better than telling an out and out lie. Everything he'd said so far was the absolute truth. Pretty much so anyhow. And he had sure enough roped the gelding out of the bunch instead of the mare.

As for whether it was a mistake or not . . . that was something he'd just as soon not commit himself to to Mr. Becker, not in so many words.

Mr. Knorr sent Benny back to the remuda and went to get his own horse. It was time they got to riding, combing the line of low hills here to find and chase down onto the prairie any cows that were hiding in the brush up there.

Mr. Becker hung back for a moment. When the others were out of hearing, he turned to Johnny and said, "I know it's a lark to twist a tenderfoot's tail, Johnny, but that young man over there really could have been hurt. Don't be doing anything like that again. You hear?"

"Yes, sir. I hear you." So he hadn't got away with his prank completely clean. But he'd got away with it. More or less.

"Don't be doing it again, John."

"No, sir. You can count on it." Which was as close to being an outright admission as Johnny wanted to come.

"I'll take your word on that, son."

"Yes, sir, thank you."

"Fine. Now get back on that horse and let's all of us go to work."

Johnny grinned and climbed onto his saddle. Chasing cows out of cover and making them do what he wanted instead of what their nature told them . . . that was the most fun part of the cow business that there was.

17

Johnny caught pure hell once they got back from the end-of-summer roundup. Got it from all sides.

Now you would think that after six days of hard work a fellow should be able to count on a little understanding if not actual sympathy. But then Johnny's mom was not in the sympathy business.

"John Harold Ackerman, whatever in the world is the matter with you? You should know better than to do a dumb thing like this. Look at those feet. Just look at them."

"I can't see them from this angle, Mama, I . . ."

"Don't you sass back at me, young man. Don't you say a word. These wrappings look like they haven't been changed since . . . John Harold, they *haven't* been changed, have they? No, don't try and deny it. I can see with my own eyes. You haven't touched them in all this time.

What were you *thinking* of? No, don't answer that. You haven't been thinking. That is the whole problem here. You probably haven't had a single thought enter that thick head of yours since your father took you off and left all the work for me to do back here at the house. Oh!"

She wrinkled her nose and made the awfulest face Johnny ever did see when she began unwrapping his feet.

Not that he could blame her. His feet — to put it bluntly — stank. They smelled sort of like rotten meat.

"Good God!" his mom exclaimed. "I just hope . . . I don't think this is gangrene. But it comes close. Oh, my." She began to cry.

That, his mother's bawling, made Johnny feel lower than the thought of losing his feet did. Well, sort of.

She really did get his attention in a big way when she mentioned gangrene. That was what took old Mr. Truax's leg back during the war. Lord knows Johnny and all the other younger fellows had heard that story often enough. It wasn't something Johnny wanted to experience for himself.

But who would've thought that going a lousy few days without changing his bandages could do harm? He wouldn't have believed it. Until now, that is. Now the smell that was underneath those linen wrappings was enough to make him believe it, want to or not.

"I can tell you one thing, young man," his mother snapped. "You won't be going anywhere for a spell." She finished the unwrapping and drew a basin of hot water from the reservoir on the side of the range.

She got a clean cloth to wash him with and one of her best towels, and pulled a stool over to the foot of the bed where Johnny was stretched out.

"You're going to spend this afternoon with these feet soaking in Epsom salts, and then I'll coat them with some of that salve your father uses to heal up cuts on the livestock. Maybe that will help you some."

"You can't put that on me, Mama. It'll burn like fire." Johnny knew some of what went into that concoction. His father started with patent-horse liniment from the store and added tar and lard and pepper and Lord knows what-all else in order to make the messy stuff.

"Good," his mother said, just as serious as could be. "It will serve you right if it does."

"But Mama . . ."

"Don't you 'but Mama' me, young man.

90

Now lie still while I go get your daddy's tin of salve. Don't you move, do you hear me?"

"Yes, ma'am. I won't. But don't forget, Mama, I have to be ready tomorrow morning to —"

"Don't even think about it, John Harold. You aren't going anywhere until these feet are better."

"But Mama . . ."

"The men can take those cows to market without you, thank goodness."

"But Mama . . ."

"Hush!"

Johnny hushed, all right. He hadn't any choice in the matter, not when his mother used that tone of voice.

But he felt sick to his stomach at the thought of having to stay here at the house while practically every other grown male human person in the entire basin went off with the culls to sell them and earn the money to carry them through the coming winter.

Driving their beeves to market was about as big a thing as the roundup, and only the young ones stayed back from it. The youngsters, and now Johnny Ackerman too.

Damn, damn, *damn!*

91

His mother came back with the flat tin of dark, smelly paste and began slathering it onto the bottoms of Johnny's feet.

All thoughts about cows and cow drives were burned completely out of his head once that fiery, awful stuff began searing the rot out of his flesh, and he let out a whoop they probably could hear all the way in town.

Whatever *had* he been thinking of for this past week, dammit all anyhow?

18

He was able to walk. It just hurt like crazy, that was all. His mama tried to keep him in bed to heal up, but that wasn't too successful. Maybe if she'd had chains and padlocks? She settled for keeping him at home so she could put the salve on fresh each morning and change the wrappings.

Actually, it wasn't as bad as it might have been. At least by being there Johnny could take care of the chores that needed doing. He hated the thought of his mother having to do all that when both him and his pop were away, so as much as he enjoyed going along for the roundups, and now the drive to market, he liked being able to do the choring while his father was away.

There weren't so many horses needed for driving a slow-moving herd, a couple spare mounts for each man was all, which meant the rest of the Rafter A saddle stock could be turned loose in the fenced horse trap below the corral. They could graze there so long as somebody kept water in the trough for them, which meant there was that much more work to do now that the roundup was over and all the light stock was back.

The heavy-bodied wagon team was in the smaller separate corral where they were kept close to hand, and of course they had to be watered too and fed grass hay since they weren't free to go find it for themselves.

The family kept a couple pigs in a pen as well. Those made their living off table scraps and garden leavings. In another month or so, after Johnny's dad got back home, they would slaughter the pigs — which were about big enough to be considered hogs at this point — and put them into the smokehouse. His mama would set up the grinder and make the sage-flavored sausage mat Johnny loved so dearly, and there would be bacon, ham, chops.

When he fed the pigs, he'd scratch them behind their ears or at the base of their tails, which near about caused them to swoon with delight, and coo sweet words to them. Like: "You're gonna taste so good." Or: "There's nothing better than hog jowl, hotcakes, and corn syrup, right, buddy?"

His mama got all gooseflesh and exasperated when he did that. She couldn't see how a body could get friendly with something and act almost like it was a pet, then turn around and have it for Sunday dinner.

Every spring, though, his pop bought two pigs to feed out over the summer, and every year Johnny would name one of them Bacon and the other Porkchop. His mama couldn't see the fun in that.

They didn't keep chickens, though. When they'd first moved up to Montana and took up this land, his mama had tried and tried to raise chickens, for she did like her eggs and all the recipes eggs are used in, but they'd never been able to keep any long enough to reach laying age.

In Kansas there had been hawks to contend with, but his mama always managed to have her chickens. Here there were hawks, owls, foxes, weasels, coyotes, and heaven knows what else carrying off the young chicks. His mother gave up on her hens after a couple of frustrated years on the undeveloped prairie.

Johnny slowly limped through his chores,

which mostly consisted of pumping and carrying water, then went back inside for breakfast.

"All done?"

"Yes, ma'am."

"Wash your hands. The biscuits are almost ready."

Johnny grinned. "With gravy?" His mama made a fine gravy using lard and white flour and some of that condensed milk like you got in cans and could keep without a springhouse.

His mother smiled and nodded. She knew it was his favorite. Well, one of his favorites. He had a good many of those. "Go on. Get washed."

"Yes'm."

"After you eat I'll change those dressings on your feet, then I want you to go in and get me some coal." When they first arrived and his folks were struggling to get the place started, they used to burn twists of dry grass. Johnny remembered that because, as little as he was then, it had been his job to make the twists. He could still do it too if need be. He remembered exactly how.

"Do you know what day of the week this is?" he asked.

"Of course, it's . . ." She stopped for a

moment to think, then shrugged and shook her head. "No. I don't."

"Me neither."

He was hoping, of course, that it was either Saturday or Sunday so Sarah wouldn't be in school mooning over that fancy boy.

Dang Foster hadn't got hurt out there on the roundup, hadn't broken any bones or anything, but once he came off Mr. Wansutter's roan he never got back onto any horse again. Not Becky's nor Sarah's nor any of the string he'd been loaned. He insisted on riding in the wagon after that, the yellow-bellied priss. Johnny hadn't liked the fellow before. Now he had contempt for the Easterner to go along with that dislike.

"I'll go hitch the team now," he suggested.

"No, those biscuits are ready to come out of the oven. You can do that later. Wash now. I'll have breakfast on the table by the time you're done."

"Yes, ma'am." He hustled outside as fast as his hurting feet could carry him.

19

The town was pretty much empty with most of the men away driving cattle. He saw a couple women on the street, Mrs. Jameson and Mrs. Truax, and further down the street a lady he didn't recognize because she was wearing a bonnet and he couldn't see her face.

The door to Mr. Perkins's shop was open. Johnny could see him in there alone with his barber chair laid back and him in it. He looked like he was asleep, and didn't look up when Johnny rumbled past in the wagon.

Johnny drove on down to Mr. Hemple's livery, which did most of its business selling hay and coal. A body would think if he was going to handle those things he would also offer grain and seed and the like, but Mr. Hanson carried those at his ranch supply store. Johnny had sometimes wondered how the two of them came up with that division, but they seemed happy enough with it and so were their customers.

"Good morning, Johnny." Mr. Hemple seemed pleased enough with an excuse to set his pitchfork aside. He was cleaning out his stalls, loading the fouled straw and manure onto a cart. When he was done, he would add it to the big pile out back, and come next spring would sell the rotted manure to folks who were putting their gardens in.

"G'morning, sir." Johnny stayed on the seat of the wagon. "Be all right if I pull around back and get a couple sacks of coal, please? Mama said you should put it onto our bill if you don't mind." The bills, here and at the mercantile and wherever else they'd done any business over the summer, would all be settled up when Johnny's pop got back with the money from selling their culls.

Hemple nodded. "Fine. Do you need any help loading the coal?"

"I can handle it, sir."

"Your feet are doing better, are they?"

Johnny couldn't believe it. Did everybody in the basin know about him messing up his feet? On second thought, yes. They almost certainly did. "They're better enough that I can get around. Sort of," he said.

"Drive around, son, and stay on that seat there. I can bring the coal out to you."

"I don't want. . . ."

"Nonsense. It's no bother at all. Go on now. Do what I say."

"Yes, sir. Thank you."

Mr. Hemple stabbed the pitchfork into the mound of manure piled on his hand-cart and left it there with the handle sticking up in the air. He went on inside the barn, and Johnny turned the wagon around and drove around to the side. By the time he got there Mr. Hemple was already standing outside with a hundred-pound sack of coal balanced on his shoulder. He brought it to the side of the wagon and tipped it into the bed. The coal landed with a thump that bounced the wagon on its springs.

"You say you need two?"

"On second thought, sir, I think maybe we'll settle for just the one bag right now. I, uh, I can come back for another one later on if she needs it."

Mr. Hemple laughed. "Any excuse, right?"

Johnny pretended not to know what he meant by that.

"You'd best heal fast, Johnny. We'll be

having another dance after everyone gets back from the drive."

"Oh, I don't dance, sir. I don't know how."

Hemple smiled. "Man doesn't have to dance just because he's at one. He can always look."

"Yes, sir, I suppose so."

"Now if you ever want to learn how, I'd say you should see if you can get that new schoolmaster to teach you. He's a young fellow that knows how to cut a figure with the ladies. Take my advice. Get the schoolmaster to teach you."

"Yes, sir. Thank you." That would be the dang day, Johnny thought glumly.

He told Mr. Hemple good-bye and made an extra wide swing around so he could get pointed back up the street. Wide enough that he could get a look over to the schoolhouse out behind the business district. The doors and windows were open and he thought he could see some movement inside, but there was no one outside on the benches or teeter-totter, no sign of Sarah or any of the older girls. Dammit.

Johnny stopped at the mercantile to get a poke of horehound candies from Mr. Archer. He'd run out while they were out gathering cows, and he sorely missed the flavor. He popped one in his mouth quick and poured a full scoop of the sweets onto the scale. While Mr. Archer was weighing the horehounds and marking down the amount to go onto the Ackerman family's tab, Johnny went behind the counter to admire the pair of handsome rifles sitting on a rack there.

Oh, they were fine-looking things. Winchester Model of 1876 in .45–60 caliber. The big rifles were known as the Montana Bear Rifle, and probably because of that name Mr. Archer had ordered two of them right after he opened his store. The rifles had been sitting unsold on the rack ever since. Pretty as they were with their handsome polished buttstocks and gleaming new actions and blued barrels, no one around here had the least use for a high-powered gun like these. Mr. Archer probably sold a dozen shotguns during the time those rifles sat useless on his rack, untouched except for having to be cleaned every so often to keep the dust off them.

They were pretty, though.

"Put your initials on this slip for me please, John."

"Yes, sir. Mr. Archer, would you mind telling me something?"

"If I can, certainly."

"I've kind of lost track, sir. Could you tell me what day of the week this would be? My mama will want to come in to church and she can't recall what the day is either."

Archer smiled. "It's Thursday."

Johnny nodded. That was a good thing to know. And two days would be just about perfect timing for him to come back and get another sack of coal and maybe some other things.

Yep. Saturday was always a good day for coming to town. And Sunday, well, his mama was pretty much sure to want to go to services now that Johnny could get around so good.

He figured he would suggest just that soon as he got home.

"Thank you, Mr. Archer."

"Nothing else for you today, Johnny?"

"No, sir. I have everything I need for right now." Johnny stuffed the twist of paper containing his candies down into a pocket and limped back out to the wagon. He was sure his mama wouldn't mind if he came back to town on Saturday. Just for, well, whatever.

20

Johnny finished hitching the team and led them over close to the door. He went inside to say good-bye to his mother.

"Wait a minute. Here's a list of things you can pick up while you're in town, son. Just give the list to Mr. Archer. He can fill the order while you're getting that other sack of coal. Although why in the world you didn't just go ahead and get it the other day I don't know. It isn't like you want an excuse to meet your friends and go on a tear with them. Everyone else is down south with the cattle."

"Yes, ma'am."

"Or is there someone else you want to see instead of the boys?" she asked, the twinkle in her eye belying the seriousness of her tone.

"No, I just . . . you know."

She laughed. "Never mind, dear. I don't want to embarrass you by asking too many questions. Mind you get back at a decent hour, though. I need the starch on that list so I can get your collar ready for church tomorrow."

"Yes'm."

"Very well then. Give me a kiss, and you can go."

He started for the door.

"Johnny?"

"Yes, ma'am?"

"If you happen to see Sarah Young please tell her hello from me."

Johnny wasn't sure, but he could feel a little heat in his ears and thought he might be blushing again. He stuffed the shopping list into his pocket and hurried out to the wagon.

"John Ackerman, you should be ashamed of yourself."

"But . . ."

"Don't tell me no buts, Johnny. I heard what you did to poor Mr. Foster."

"But I . . ."

"Be quiet. I know. And I know you did it a'purpose too. I heard all about it." Sarah had her fists planted on her hips and her expression was enough to curdle milk. She was bright red in the face, except for a rim of white around her mouth where she'd clamped her lips so hard together. Johnny was scared fire and lightning were going to come leaping out of her eyes and stab him right through the heart, she was that mad.

"He could have been hurt, you know. He could have been *killed*. But you didn't think about that, did you? Well, did you? Did you think before you put him all unsuspecting on that mean old horse? Did you?"

"Well, I, uh . . ." He stammered and backed away a couple steps. What the heck could he say to something like that anyway? No, I didn't think about it; I'm an idiot? Or, of course I thought about it, but it's okay if the dang schoolteacher gets thrown and stomped and busted all to pieces? Sarah wasn't being fair. Not at all fair.

"You should be ashamed, Johnny. I'm ashamed for you."

Not a word of sympathy or concern about him. Foster came off that horse and bounced and got up as hale and healthy as when he hit the dang ground. Johnny was the one who could've lost his feet to the gangrene. Could have walked around on two stumps the rest of his life. But did Sarah care about that? No, sir, he reckoned she did not.

All she cared about now was that damn schoolmaster.

"I got t' go," Johnny mumbled. "I got to get some coal for my mom."

He left Sarah standing in the aisle there and scampered outside. He could come back to Archer's store later to pick up the things his mama wanted.

He was mad when he left, though. He'd come all the way back to town now mostly so he would have a chance to run into Sarah on the weekend day when there wasn't any school in session.

But did she care? Did she care the least little bit about him?

She did not. And wasn't that for damn sure.

Johnny was feeling almighty sorry for himself when he went back outside and drove down to the livery. He wished he'd gone ahead and gotten the coal Thursday when he was in town so he didn't have to come back today.

21

Johnny wished now he hadn't found out what day it was. Or at least that he hadn't told his mom. If she hadn't known it was Sunday morning, he could have avoided driving her to church services. As it was, he was trapped.

He dawdled and grumbled with the horses and harness, but there was no getting around it. His mother had been baking and preparing since before daybreak, and there was nothing short of a prairie fire that would keep her from going now. Come to think of it, if there was a fire, she would probably just insist that he drive around it so she could join everyone else in praying that it do no harm.

It seemed strange to be going without his pop along. Johnny noticed his mother was packing just as much in the lunch basket as she always did, so maybe this was a little odd for her too.

"Is everything ready outside?"

"Yes'm. I brought the wagon around."

She picked up the heavy basket. "Hold the door for me, please."

"I can get it, Mama."

"No, dear. Your feet . . ."

"Mama, my feet are way better. Honest. Now let me get that." He took the basket from her and carried it out and slid it into the wagon, then lifted the tailgate and latched it in place. He helped his mother onto the box, then unclipped the hitching weights from the horses' bits and dropped them onto the floor before climbing in and taking up the driving lines.

"I feel like I've forgotten something," she said.

Johnny laughed. "Mama, you say that every time we go someplace. You've never forgot anything yet."

"That's what your father says too."

"I know." Johnny shook out the lines to get the horses' attention, then snapped the buggy whip over their ears — not too close or his pop would have *his* ears for breakfast — and they rolled and jolted away from the yard.

22

Johnny didn't think he had ever been more miserable in his whole life. When they were singing, that darned fancy-boy schoolteacher stood so close behind Sarah it was a wonder he didn't have his nose buried in her hair.

And Johnny could see that she'd done herself up extra special too. She had her hair fixed different from the way she usually did. It was braided. That was ordinary enough; she often did that. But this time her hair was braided . . . he didn't know what it was called, but it was a thicker, shinier, *different* sort of look. Not the pigtails like she wore when she was littler, nor the skinny braid that sometimes hung down her back. This one was fatter and shorter and kind of fancy.

He probably would have liked this way of doing it except for thinking who it was made up fancy for. Not him, that was for sure.

Foster had gone and turned himself out special too. Instead of a string tie like gentlemen would normally wear, he had one of those puffy, old-fashioned ties. Except this one, dang him, somehow didn't look old-fashioned at all. It was silk, bright red, and had a gaudy stickpin jabbed into the middle of the knot. Johnny could think of better places for the pin to go.

To make it all the worse, the schoolteacher and Sarah stepped out away from the rest of the choir and sang a duet together, just the two of them singing aco . . . aca . . . without any music.

He wondered how many hours they'd practiced their duet.

When they were done Foster bowed and Sarah curtsied, first to the congregation and then to each other. The sight of the two of them preening and posturing right there in front of the whole community made Johnny sick.

He didn't hear another word Mr. Tolliver had to say for the rest of the service, and when they broke for lunch later, he took his mother by the elbow and tugged her away from the clutch of hens who generally cackled together. All of Johnny's friends were off with the cows so if he'd been going to visit with anybody, it would only have been the girls and the young kids. And Ed Foster.

"Mama, d'you think it would be all right if we was to go back home now?"

"What's wrong, dear? Are you sick? Are your feet hurting you?"

"I'm all right. I just . . . I'd like to go home, that's all."

She dug a little lace trimmed handkerchief out of a pocket and wet one corner of it with spit, then scrubbed a spot beside his left eye. Johnny hated it when she did that. Then she pressed the back of her hand against his forehead to check to see if he had a temperature. He didn't. So she tried again on the side of his neck, as if she'd find one there even though there wasn't any on his forehead.

She peeled the skin down under one eye and then the other and peered close at the whites.

Finally she shook her head. "You're sick, aren't you. You don't want to say anything, but I can tell. A mother knows these things."

"Can we go home now, Mama? Please?"

She sighed. "Yes. Let me drop off some of this food to share. Then we can go home."

"Thank you, Mama."

Johnny didn't look to see where Foster and Sarah had gotten to. He didn't really want to know.

23

It was another three weeks, almost four, before his pop got home. Johnny didn't go anyplace that entire time, not to church, and to town only once. That was to pick up some flour and saleratus that his mother said she needed. Then he only drove in, went to the store, and came straight back home again without stopping to visit. Didn't even take time to moon over the new saddles down at Hanson's Ranch Supply.

Of course he did add a poke of horehound candies to their order at Archer's, but that didn't take any extra time as he already had to be there for the other things.

His father came home smiling, and Johnny hurried out to tend to the horses so his pop could get inside quick and give his mother the hugging that he would have been missing out on while he was away.

"You're moving good," his father said. "Your feet all better now?"

"Yes, sir, they're healed up."

"Learn anything from that, did you?"

Johnny laughed. "Maybe. Or maybe not."

"Well, at least you're honest." His father reached over and mussed Johnny's hair, just like he used to when Johnny was little. "It's good to see you, son. Good to be back home."

"Did you do all right with the buyers?"

"We'll be able to keep you in flapjacks and syrup this whole fall and winter if that's what you're asking." His pop winked at him, then said, "Truth is, the market price is good this year. Best I've ever seen. We were all grinning on the ride home. Know what I'm going to do with some of it?"

Johnny shook his head.

"Can you keep a secret?"

"From who?"

"From your mama."

"Oh, I've been able to keep secrets from you and her since I was this high." He leaned down and made a hand motion about knee level.

"Not as many as you might think you were keeping. But that isn't the point." His father threw his bedroll over his shoulder while Johnny loosened the cinches on his old saddle. "The thing is, on my way through town I stopped at Archer's. You know that fancy hat your mother has been admiring?"

Johnny smiled. "You didn't."

"I surely did. Put the order in and paid down cash in full. And a pretty new ribbon sash to go with it."

"A ribbon, do you mean? Or a sash?"

"Damned if I know exactly. It's called a ribbon sash, and this one is the same color as the trimmings on that hat. They say it's all the rage in Paris."

"Paris, Texas?"

His pop laughed. "That too for all I know. The only thing I care about is that your mama likes it."

"So what did you bring me, huh?"

"What? Are you getting greedy?"

"Just remembering how it used to be when you'd go off someplace. You always brought back some little something, even if it was only a little chunk of wood you'd whittle into a toy for me. I remember how you used to do that. It meant a lot to me. Not so much what you brought, but that you took the bother."

"You never told me that before, son."

"Reckon you never asked. But you're evading the question. What'd you bring me home this time?"

"Brought you a twist of those horehound candies you like so much, how's that."

"Thanks, Pop. I do dearly love those. Thank you."

His father opened one side of his saddlebags, looked inside, and turned it around to open the other. What he pulled out was no poke of horehounds, though. He handed Johnny a little box wrapped in brown paper and tied off with string.

"What is it?"

"Open it up and see for yourself, why don't you."

The horses and gear were just going to have to wait another couple minutes in the yard here. Johnny used his pocketknife to slice the string, then hastily ripped the paper off. His mother would have laboriously untied the string and unfolded the paper so both could be used again. But then she had more patience than he did.

"Papa! Oh, my. Is it . . . is this really for me?"

"Figured it was about time to had one of your own," his father said. "So you'll quit pestering me with questions whenever you want to know."

Johnny lifted the watch out of the box as if it was more fragile than fine china.

It was probably the most beautiful watch there had ever been. It had a silver case with an engraved scene showing a calf at the end of a rope. The case was flat and sleek, not the old turnip style of watchcases. And it was a stem-wind model too that didn't need a separate key.

"The man said to mind you don't wind it too tight. And he said it's best if you decide on a time of day and stick with that so you won't forget and lose track. First thing in the morning maybe or else last thing at night before you sleep. Just wind it once each day, not so tight you bust the spring, and it should serve you and your son after you."

"Thanks, Papa." Johnny threw his arms around his father's neck. Then, realizing, blushed and stepped back a little.

His pop smiled and came forward and went ahead and hugged him right back.

Johnny hadn't expected that. But then his dad probably hadn't either. It was nice, though. Felt good.

"I, uh, I better get these horses cleaned up and bedded down. And I bet Mama is getting impatient. She saw you ride in." Johnny grinned. "You should've seen the dust fly when she got to scurrying around setting the table just so and clanging pot lids."

"All right. Good." Lewis Ackerman took a few steps toward the house.

"Pop."

"Yes, son?"

"I'm glad you're safe to home."

"Me too, son. Me too." Then his father picked up his pace into a trot. He was running by the time he got to the door where, by then, Johnny's mom was standing with her hands clutched inside a fold of apron and a wetness in her eyes.

24

"Now would you look what the cat drug in," Johnny said, leaning against the fence rails and looking up at Pipper and Andy and Curtis Upshaw, who were all still mounted. "Have a good drive, did you?"

"You should've been there," Andy said.

"Don't I know it."

"Anything happen while we were away?"

Johnny shook his head. Certainly nothing had happened that he wanted to talk about. For that matter, it was true that nothing had happened. Mostly.

"Well something's happening now," Pipper told him.

Johnny lifted an eyebrow and waited for Pipper to spill whatever it was that brought them all the way out here.

"Saturday a week is gonna be the hayride."

Johnny started to grin. Then thought better of it. He loved the hayrides they had every fall. Always had until this year anyhow.

Each fall Mr. Hemple brought out his big old freight wagon, the trailer too, and loaded it high with hay, then hitched his heaviest draft horses to it. All the young people in the basin, the kids and the half-growns and the pretty-much-growns like Johnny and his friends, they all piled in and rode a good four hours south of town to Mr. James Woollet's farm.

Every year Woollet put in a pumpkin patch with just this in mind. They'd ride down in the afternoon and get there in time so there was enough daylight left that the little kids could run out in the patch and choose some pumpkins to carry home with them in time for carving into jack-o'-lanterns.

Once the pumpkins were carried back to the wagon and marked as to who they belonged to, then everybody would gather around a grand bonfire that Mr. Woollet would have laid ready to light. They'd roast ears of corn and sausages dangled on sticks and drink sweet cider and then sit around and sing. It was always late before they crawled back into the hay and started the long ride back to town.

It was fun.

It was also, Johnny recalled, where he got his first kiss.

That was the year he was fifteen. The girl's name was Suzanne, and she was an older woman. Sixteen. She was kind of cute, but even if she hadn't been, well, just the idea of kissing a girl was about enough to make a fifteen-year-old bust his britches. He'd kissed her good for about half the ride back to town, the whole rest of the way home actually once they got the kissing started, and Johnny thought he was in love.

He wasn't. Or anyway Suzanne wasn't. She hadn't wanted anything much to do with him after that one night. He'd never exactly figured that out.

Not that it really mattered. The next spring she'd up and married a cowboy from Arkansas, and the two of them had moved. Oregon, he'd heard, and it could be true. He'd also heard that she was in a family way and had to get married, but that was only a rumor and Johnny never believed it. Suzanne was a nice girl, and he'd always liked her. Especially after that hayride.

But now . . .

"I ain't going this year," he heard himself say.

"Hell, Johnny, it wouldn't be the same without you. You got to come."

"Naw, I don't think so. You three can take care of it."

"Not me," Curtis put in. "I been paid off. They're only keeping a couple of the older hands on over the winter. That's why I come out here. I wanted to tell you good-bye."

"Will you be back in the spring?"

Curtis shrugged. "Depends on what turns up, I suppose. I thought I'd take a boat ride. Go down to St. Louis. They say it's something. Maybe even see can I get on as a deckhand on something going on down to N'Orleans."

"Oo-la-la. You know what they say about the women in New Orleans, don't you?" Johnny said.

"No. Do you?"

"Not me." He grinned. "But if you come up this way again next year, you can tell us."

Curtis laughed. "I'll do it too."

"Johnny, about the hayride . . ." Andy started in on him.

"No, I got my mind made up about this. Besides, the hayride is for the little kids. We're too old for that stuff."

"That isn't the way you looked at it last year."

"We're all a year older now, aren't we."

"You got to come, Johnny," Pipper insisted.

Johnny shook his head. "I reckon not. You fellas go on. Enjoy yourselves."

"Oh, we will. We just wish you'd come with us."

"Think it over," Andy said. "Mind now, it isn't this Saturday next, but the Saturday a week from this Saturday."

"Aw, we'll see him again before then. We'll talk him into it."

"Well, I won't see you again soon," Curtis said, leaning down from his saddle with his hand extended. "You're all right, Johnny. I hope we meet up again sometime."

"Me too, Curtis."

They shook hands and Johnny stepped back.

He felt . . . older somehow, but not especially happy, as he stood there by the corral fence and watched the three of them ride off.

After a bit he shook himself out of his thinking and went into the barn to get after the chores.

25

"Son, there's something I'd like you to do today."

"Sure thing, Pop." Johnny eyed the pair of leftover hotcakes on the platter in the center of the table, but decided he better leave them be. One more bite and his belly would burst wide open, and wouldn't that make an awful mess on his mama's clean floor. "What do you need?"

"I want you to ride into town and pay off our bill with Sam Archer."

"Me? You want me to do that?"

"I don't know of any reason why you couldn't," his father said. "Do you?"

Johnny grinned. "No, sir, I expect that I don't."

"I don't know how much we owe, so I'll just give you enough that I'm sure should cover it. Sam will have our slips in the drawer there. But mind that you add them up yourself."

Johnny started to say something, but his father cut him off. "Now I don't for a minute believe Sam would cheat us, not for a penny nor for a fortune. But anybody can make a mistake. So you add it up yourself after he does."

"Yes, sir."

"I'll pack you a lunch to carry along," his mother said. "Just in case it takes you a spell."

"Yes'm. Is there anything else, Pop?"

Lewis Ackerman shook his head. "I don't think of anything. You got the morning chores done already, didn't you?"

"Of course."

"In that case, all you have to do is get saddled. I'll get the cash for you to carry while Mother makes up your lunch."

Johnny was smiling when he went out to collect his gear and a horse to throw it on. His pop wasn't fooling him any.

Oh, Johnny was sure his father wanted the bill at Archer's paid. But that wasn't the only reason he was sending Johnny off on an errand. His dad wanted time alone with Johnny's mom. Now that was about the long and the short of it.

Johnny whistled as he went about getting ready to go. He'd get the errand run and then, since he'd have a lunch along

126

anyway, go waste the afternoon somehow.

Maybe go down along the creek. Or even see could he catch a fish or two. He and his father used to fish a good deal, but lately it seemed they'd gotten out of the habit. That was a shame. He'd always enjoyed going off to fish, just the two of them. They'd spent some fine hours that way.

Yeah, that was a good enough idea though even if it would be just himself. He went back inside the barn to fetch a spool of waxed harness thread — there wasn't a fish in the territory big enough to bust the thick cotton thread used for harness stitching — and the round tin that used to hold salve of some sort but that had been their fishhook repository since before Johnny could remember.

He felt like he was going off on a holiday, by golly.

26

Stupid fish! He could see them hanging there just downstream from a rock that lay at the edge of the creek bank. There were four of them. Moving their fins just enough to stay in place against the flow, lying there waiting for the water to carry a bug or something to them.

Johnny sure didn't know what exact kind of bug they were waiting for, though. He'd tried offering them everything he could catch in the grass along the bank. Grasshopper, horsefly, grub, everything he could get hold of. He'd impale the little suckers on the tip end of a hook and drop them in just above the stone where the trout were hanging and let the water carry them around the rock and the eddy swirl them in in front of the dang fishes' noses.

And then the dang creek would carry his bait right on down while the trout ignored the whole process.

Johnny was getting peeved.

Free food and the darn fish wouldn't have a bite. Stupid fish. Not worth catching either. Not really. They weren't but six, maybe eight inches long.

And anyway, he already had a lunch with him.

And he didn't like the taste of trout to begin with. His pop liked it awful well, but Johnny always thought the meat of it tasted kind of icky.

If it was meat that was on a fish's bones. He wasn't real sure about that. After all, they said the Catholics couldn't eat meat on some days — he didn't know which — but they could eat fish those times. Just like everybody else did on Good Friday. Fish was okay, but meat was not.

Which must mean that the . . . whatever you called it . . . the flesh on a trout wasn't meat at all but something else.

Johnny lay back in the shaded sweet grass and thought about that and a couple dozen equally weighty matters while his hook and bait fluttered in the water far downstream of the rock where the stupid little trout were.

The truth was that he was satisfied well enough even if he wasn't catching anything. The object of fishing isn't the fish, after all, but the fishing.

After a bit, he sat up and untied the sack that held his lunch. It was a fine day, cool and bright and cloudless. He could hear a faint murmur of moving water and a soft droning buzz as the last of the season's bugs did whatever it was bugs did to prepare for the winter soon to come. A couple rods off his horse was cropping grass, tearing it loose with that ripping sound and noisily chewing. The horse was tied on a picket rope. This particular one was bad about traveling long distances even if you put hobbles on it, so Johnny didn't trust it unless he had it tied in place. He didn't want to go on any hikes this afternoon.

He ate — cold beef and biscuits with some horehound candies for dessert — then lay down again and tipped his hat over his eyes.

The good thing about it was that he didn't have to feel the least bit guilty about taking time for himself here.

After all, his folks were having an even nicer time than he was.

27

It was late afternoon before Johnny headed home. The truth was that he'd fallen asleep and kind of lost much of the afternoon. He didn't have a single trout to show for all his hard work — well, sort of — but he did have a bunch of cattails and dried flowers to take to his mother.

At this time of year there weren't any wildflowers in bloom any longer, but she liked dried arrangements too and her old ones were getting kind of bald and scrungy-looking as the leaves and brown petals fell off over time. He thought it would please her to have these new ones from along the creek bed.

He approached town from the south, down by the livery, and rode past the businesses along Main. Wisps of smoke curled out of most of the stovepipes on both sides of the street, and the air smelled of burning coal. Wood smoke smelled a whole lot nicer than coal, but there just wasn't all that much wood available around Redhorse Butte. You had to drive and haul for an awful long way if you wanted to cut wood in this day and age, and coal was ever so much easier. Cheaper too, he supposed, when you considered the labor that would be involved trying to get wood to burn.

He was thinking about that sort of thing as he passed Archer's, and was paying no mind to the store or to anybody who might be inside it, but he was stopped by a voice calling his name.

Johnny reined the horse to a stop without thinking even though — or maybe because — he recognized the voice before he turned his head to look.

"H'lo, Sarah." He touched the brim of his hat.

Sarah was standing just inside the doorway of the mercantile. She turned her head — Lordy, but she was so awful pretty — and spoke to someone he couldn't see, then stepped out onto the sidewalk boards.

She was wearing a faded blue everyday dress and her scuffed old lace-up shoes and no bonnet, but he still thought she was pretty enough that surely she was the reason the sun came up each morning, just so the world could see her and her smile.

In spite of the way she'd ignored him ever since the fancy boy arrived, well, he couldn't help himself. He still thought she was awful special.

"Are you in a hurry?" she asked.

"No, I reckon not."

"Then could I talk to you for a minute?" She paused. "Please?"

Johnny felt the same gut-fluttering excitement he always experienced when he was around Sarah. He nodded. "Yeah, I . . . sure." He reined the horse's head around and nudged it up to the hitch rail outside the store and dismounted there.

He didn't know what she intended or how long this would take, but he supposed it wouldn't be proper to stand there in the street while Sarah said whatever it was she wanted to say, so he took a wrap around the rail with his reins and stepped up onto the boardwalk beside her. He still had his mother's dried flower bouquet in his hand and felt a little awkward holding it.

"I, uh, I picked these for my mom," he said.

"They're pretty."

"Yeah, thanks. So, um, what was it you wanted to tell me?"

"Are your feet better now? That is, can you walk all right?"

"I'm fine now."

"Could we go inside for a minute please, Johnny?"

"Sure." He took his hat off and followed Sarah into the store. The warmth coming off the cast-iron stove at the back of the store felt good. He hadn't realized until he felt the heat just how cool it was outside now that the sun was almost down.

The only customer in the place was Catherine Becker, so it must have been Catherine who Sarah spoke to a minute ago. And, of course, Mr. Archer was over by the counter. Johnny had about half-expected to see Foster there, but there was no sign of the schoolteacher. He was pleased to see that was so.

"What is it you wanted to talk to me about?" he asked when Sarah did not immediately bring it up.

She touched his elbow and pulled him away from the door and over to the side where the yard goods were. "Andy told me you aren't going on the hayride this year," she said, her voice low and her eyes large and blue and innocent.

"That's true enough."

"I was hoping. . . ." She touched him

again. On the wrist this time, below his coat sleeve. The feel of her fingertips on his skin was like she was charged with static electricity. Except there was no snap of noise nor any spark. Not the kind that can be seen anyhow. "I was hoping you would come," she said, her eyes wide open and luminous.

Johnny felt like groaning. Or maybe melting. He felt a heaviness in his chest and a lurch of excitement deep in his belly. "I . . . I . . ."

"Please?" she asked. "Can't you change your mind? You said your feet are healed now. Won't you come with us?"

"I, uh . . ."

"I would miss you if you didn't come, Johnny. Please?"

His tongue was thick. Too thick to talk around. Sarah still had her fingers on his wrist. He wanted to reach out and grab her. He wanted to turn and run.

He nodded.

Sarah broke into a broad, sweet smile. "Really? You *will* come? Thank you."

She stepped closer to him and without even looking around to see if anyone was watching, came onto her tiptoes and planted a soft, moist kiss onto his lips. Not on his cheek either. She kissed him right on the mouth, and only missed dead center by half a lip or thereabouts.

Johnny felt suddenly light-headed, as if he might pass right out and collapse full length on the mercantile floor.

"Thank you, Johnny. I'll see you there, right?"

He nodded again, too dumbfounded to speak.

Without conscious thought he shoved the bundle of cattails and dried flowers into Sarah's hands.

Sarah blinked. Johnny turned and got the heck out of there before he did something to scandalize the both of them and get the town's tongues to wagging.

He was completely out of town, all the way past Perkins's barbershop, before he had his wits about him enough to recognize where he was and what he was doing.

Nossir, he might not have caught a single fish, but this had turned out to be one of the best days of his whole life after all.

Johnny let out a whoop and put the spurs to his horse to let the animal help him run off some of the excitement that was just too much to contain.

Lordy, Lordy, oh, *my!*

28

The day was cool, just short of being cold, but Johnny was sweat-soaked and itchy. Dust and seeds from the hay got caught in the sticky sweat inside his shirt and like to drove him crazy. If there was one chore in the year's cycle of them that he purely did not like, it was this one right here, stacking hay against winter need.

Mowing the hay and turning it wasn't so awful bad, and even pitching it onto the wagon to haul it in was okay. The new-mowed hay was still green enough that it wasn't any real nuisance to handle. But by the time they got around to the stacking, the dried grasses had been thrown around enough that the stems were becoming brittle and the heads were beginning to come apart.

Dang stuff got dusty then, and putting it high up in the air like you did with the stacker was just like winnowing it so that all the loose bits were blown off. Blown all over whoever was shaping the stack and those loading the stacker, that is.

It was a funny thing. Just like cigar smoke always seeming to blow toward anybody that didn't smoke or hated the smell, the haying dust always blew from the stacker to the loaders. Johnny suspected there was a law written down about that, though he didn't know where.

One of God's little jokes, he figured. And didn't there seem to be an awful lot of those.

Johnny rested the tines of his fork on the ground and itched and scratched and watched while the big horses pushed the blade up the portable wooden ramp all the way to the top, fifteen feet or so high. The blade reached the top and the load of hay in front of it tipped over the edge and fell onto the pile below, where a couple of the younger fellows then stepped in and got busy arranging the pile so it wouldn't fall apart when the next batch was dropped.

Shaping the stack like they were doing under the supervision of Johnny's dad was even dustier and itchier work than loading the sweep, so he supposed that standing on bare ground and tossing forkfuls of hay onto the ramp wasn't so bad after all.

Quick as a load of hay was dropped off the top of the tall ramp, Mr. Hemple backed his team away, letting the sweep down to ground level again so it could be reloaded and the horses driven forward to push that batch up and dump it onto the growing stack.

Mr. Hemple always insisted on using his own team of heavy drafters, and he always drove them himself too. But then the stacker was his, the only one in the basin, and they all hired the use of it, turn and turn about, those who went to the trouble to put hay up anyway. There were a few outfits, like Adam Johnson, who relied on whatever graze or forage could be found naturally to get his stock through the winters. The farmers and nowadays most of the ranchers too cut hay and put it by.

Johnny's dad said, if nothing else, it was better to have the horses kept close to the house so they were always available when they were needed, and a man had to feed stored hay if he wanted to do that once the naturally cured prairie grasses were buried deep in snow. By the end of winter an animal would have to wander pretty far in order to find graze for itself.

Horses would paw their way through the snow in order to find something to eat.

Cows were too stupid to do that, so Lewis Ackerman and most of the others tended to put up all the hay they could as an emergency reserve in case the winter was a bad one. Johnny stood there enjoying the beauty and the power of Mr. Hemple's big, dark gray draft horses. They had some Percheron blood in them and were almighty handsome.

Once they backed far enough that the hay sweep was down on the ground and Mr. Hemple dropped the reins so the horses would know to stand waiting, Johnny and Andy, who was helping out for the day, jumped to work again loading the sweep ready to shove another load onto the top of the stack they were building.

Dang hay dust and seeds and junk had gotten all the way past the bandanna at his throat and the tight-buttoned shirt collar and was all the way down to his waist at this point. Johnny threw a fork of hay onto the ramp, scratched his itching belly, and threw some more hay on.

In a couple minutes this bunch would be ready and Mr. Hemple would push it up the ramp. Johnny and Andy would stand there and get chilled while they waited for the sweep to be brought back down again. It was a pureantee wonder they every one of them didn't catch some sort of epizootic from standing out here working up a sweat in the cold every haying time.

Mr. Hemple clucked to his team and the big boys leaned into their harness, powerful muscles rippling under sleek hides. A big horse hard at work, that was about as pretty a thing as a body could ever see.

Well, short of Sarah Young anyway. But there was something might pretty about a good horse too.

Johnny set the tines of his fork down onto the ground and worked his hand inside his shirt to scratch another itch. Over on the other side of the ramp, Andy was doing the same thing.

29

Johnny carried water until his arms ached, and he brought in two extra buckets of coal. He filled the reservoir on the side of the big cast-iron range and stoked the fire until it began to purr.

"It isn't all that cold today, son, but if you're really chilly you should put your fire in the potbelly and not in your mama's cookstove, don't you think?"

"Lewis Ackerman, hush that teasing now. You know good and well the hayride is tonight and he'll be wanting a bath before he goes."

Johnny gave his mom a grateful look. And tried to avoid glancing over at his dad, who would be peering over the top of the book he'd been reading, grinning fit to beat the band.

"Is that tonight? My goodness, I'd forgotten."

Johnny could hear the smile in his father's voice.

"Yes, sir, a person never knows what-all might happen on a hayride," Lewis rattled on. "Remember the hayride back home, Stella? You know the one I mean. That was the first time you and me . . ."

"Lewis!"

His father didn't say anything more. But then he didn't really have to.

Johnny looked around then. His dad had that look on him, sort of a cat-that-ate-the-canary look. Smug but happy too. And his mom didn't look at all put out, never mind her screeching to stop his father from saying anything more. In fact, she looked every bit as pleased as his father at the memories of some hayride from years and years back.

Johnny smiled too, then added another quart of coal to the firebox and went outside and around to the back of the house where they kept the washtub hanging on a peg. If you didn't bring it in soon enough to warm it up before you used it, the cold metal would take all the heat out of the water and you'd end up having a chilly bath.

30

Lordy, but Sarah was pretty. This afternoon she was wearing what looked like a spanking-new dress, sort of a cream color, all starched and ironed crisp, and she had golden yellow ribbons in her hair and pure white stockings — which he could see because of the way the hem of her dress pulled up when she settled into the hay — and shoes that were polished so that there wasn't a single smudge or scuff mark anyplace on them. She looked bright as a new penny, he thought.

But then he would've thought that if she'd just stepped out of a mud bog. He admitted that to himself.

Johnny and his pals perched atop the deepest part of the pile, up close to the front of the wagon, while Sarah and the other girls of middling age occupied the middle and the little kids were closest to the tailgate. On the ride back after dark, that distribution was apt to change a little. It always did. Johnny just hoped . . . well, she'd come right out and asked him to be there, hadn't she? He had good reason to be optimistic.

Cold as the nights were getting, the day was almost warm lying there in the afternoon sunshine, and despite his excitement Johnny felt lazy-eyed and sleepy while the rumble of the wagon and the softness of the hay kind of rocked and lulled him. It was a nice feeling. Comforting, sort of. It occurred to him as he rode that this would probably be the last year it was appropriate for him to come along on the hayride. He was getting too old for it. Another year and he would likely be looking back on the hayrides as a part of his childhood.

It would soon be time, he realized, for him to be giving some thought to the future. Soon time to consider where he wanted to be. And doing what. And with who.

Whom, he corrected himself. With whom.

He lifted his head and tipped his hat back off his eyes and looked down toward the middle of the wagon bed to where the girls were.

With whom indeed.

Johnny tilted his hat back over his eyes

and smiled a little as he lay back into the comfort of the soft hay.

It was early yet. He didn't have to be making any decisions right now.

But he did have a good idea of what direction he wanted to take. Someday.

31

Mr. Woollet had outdone himself this year. There were the usual roasting ears, soaked in a tub of salted water for more than a day and then buried over top of a bed of coals for the entire day of the hayride. And the fat, stubby sausages that Mr. Perkins made whenever anybody had a tough old bull that needed to be replaced with new or younger blood.

Tough as they were, the bulls had a wonderful flavor when they were ground up fine and the meat mixed with locally gathered sage and spices from faraway places and God knows what-all else. Mr. Perkins was the town's butcher as well as its barber. He had a smokehouse behind his shop, and that added to the flavor of the sausages too. There wasn't hardly anything better than his sausages.

And this year Mr. Woollet added a huge basket full of tarts to be passed out for everybody. Johnny didn't know who'd baked them. Maybe Mr. Woollet, though Johnny doubted that. The farmer was a widower and had no wife, although it could be he was taking up with some woman and keeping the fact hid. Whatever and whoever, the tarts looked mighty fine. Johnny was anxious to sample a few to see what kind they were, but the basket was not to be touched until after they'd eaten.

The little kids went scampering off to the pumpkin patch to make their selections. The middling-sized ones went along to help with cutting and carrying the bright orange treasures. The older girls clucked and fussed and got everything laid out on the long plank and bench tables that were already set up, and the older boys attended to the serious business of lighting the bonfire that Mr. Woollet had ready.

It was fine, really fine, and the little ones had their pumpkins in the wagon before full dark.

By then the older boys had a batch of sausages already roasted for the little ones. They did that so there couldn't be any danger of one of the small ones taking a tumble into the fire, which had almost happened the first year Mr. Woollet and

Mr. Hemple staged the hayride and feast. It was considered something of a growing-up when a kid, boy or girl either one, was allowed to roast his own sausage links.

The corn had been dug up and the ears, wrapped in crisp, heat-browned husks, tumbled into a big tub. There were pots of sweet butter on the tables, and little brushes to paint the corn with once the husks were stripped away.

The girls oversaw getting the little ones settled and fed, then the rest could dig in and eat too.

Once everybody was stuffed near to the point of bursting their bellies wide open, they left the tables and stood around the bonfire. That was supposed to be so they could keep warm in the chill of the evening, but even when the fall was a warm one, they did it anyway so they could stand in the firelight and sing and maybe do some whispering about who was going to ride where when the time came for everybody to climb into the hay wagon again.

At one point Johnny glanced over to his right, and there was Sarah standing close beside him.

She looked up with those huge, innocent, wide-open eyes and smiled at him. Johnny like to melted right down into the ground, then and there.

"Have you promised to ride with anybody yet?" she whispered. She had to lift herself onto tiptoe to reach his ear to whisper into, and she kept her balance by putting her hand on his shoulder. She put her lips so close to his ear that he could feel her breath warm on his cheek. Johnny felt a tingle of excitement when she did that and a fullness in his groin.

"Well, have you?"

He shook his head, his ability to speak wiped away for just a moment or two there.

"Would you ride with me?" Her whisper was so soft he barely heard it. Could scarcely believe what he thought she said.

"Ye . . . yes."

He felt her squeeze his shoulder, then she was gone. The next time he looked, he spotted a pale flash of her dress as she moved through the shadows behind the kids, slipping around to the other side of the fire.

Johnny moaned just a little, although he couldn't tell for sure if he'd done it out loud or only thought to.

He tugged his new watch out of his pocket and wondered just how long it would be until Mr. Hemple decided it was time to head back to town.

Too much time, that was for sure.

But he could wait. He had to.

Johnny felt like letting out a war whoop, but he knew better lest Andy and Pipper guess what was up and rib him about it.

But oh . . . oh . . . he wished he could set his watch ahead and get the bonfire singing over with so they could start back to Redhorse Butte.

32

Johnny helped get the little kids settled all snug and sleepy with their pumpkins at their sides. Then he sort of nonchalantly followed Sarah onto the hay to one side of the wagon, kind of out of the way.

Out of the corner of his eye he saw that Andy was doing the same thing on the other side, except with Becky Wannsutter. For about half a second Johnny felt a flash of anger with Andy. There'd been a time when Johnny sort of thought of Becky as his girlfriend and he was pretty sure she'd felt the same. Of course that was a spell back, and it wasn't any longer so, but he could feel that pang of resentment anyway. Johnny had no interest in old Becky, not really, and he was pleased for Andy. Of course he was. But for just that half second . . .

Any thoughts he might have been having along those lines were wiped away when

Sarah wriggled down into the hay. It was pretty thoroughly dark now that the fire was dying down and there wasn't yet any moon showing, but he could see a glimpse of white stocking above her shoe tops. Cold as it was, he could feel himself begin to sweat, and he was breathing hard when he burrowed in beside her.

"I'm cold," Sarah announced first thing when they had themselves a nest of sorts dug into the soft, sweet-smelling hay.

For a moment there Johnny thought she meant to change her mind, but that wasn't it at all. She gave him an impish look and in a mock-serious tone of voice added, "I think what we ought to do, Johnny, is for you to cover us with your coat. Then we can put my cloak over top of both of us, and we'll be covered over as complete as a pair of prairie dogs in their own little den. Don't you think?" Her eyes were quite innocent, but the sparkle in them was not.

Johnny was out of his coat lickety-split. He spread it wide over top of both of them and put Sarah's cloak over them too.

Sarah tugged her cloak high so their heads were covered as well as the rest of them. That left their feet and lower legs out in the cold. Johnny didn't mind that even a little bit, though.

153

What little light there had been was obscured now with his coat and her woolen cloak pulled over their heads.

"I'm cold on this side over here, Johnny. Can you get a little closer, do you think?"

He could.

"That's much better now, thank you." Her voice was a faint whisper. He could smell the scent of ripe corn on Sarah's breath and could feel that breath on his chin. He slid a little lower in the hay so they were face-to-face, his right arm kind of necessarily held around her.

He could feel how slim she was and the rise and fall of her chest as she breathed. For a minute or so he was afraid Sarah would be able to feel his reaction to her nearness, but she seemed not to notice.

He swallowed back a lump in his throat and sort of experimentally laid his left hand flat on Sarah's belly. She was sure to notice that, but she didn't say anything.

Voices drifted across the hay wagon in the night. They sounded far away and indistinct.

He could hear Mr. Woollet calling good-byes and an answering chorus from the little kids in back, and the wagon jolted forward as Mr. Hemple started them back toward town.

The movement of the wagon jostled Johnny against Sarah and the next thing he knew — he honest to Pete hadn't intended it; thought about it plenty, of course, but hadn't yet decided if he should be brazen enough to try it — next thing he knew his lips were tasting of Sarah's and they were kissing.

The really amazing thing was that Sarah was kissing him back. He could feel her lips moving on his.

He rubbed her stomach with the flat of his hand, and probed between her lips with the tip of his tongue, which was something he'd heard about but never done before. He was afraid she would rear back and sock him one when he did a bold thing like that. But she never. She just continued kissing him right on back. And after a spell — he like to passed out when she did it — he could feel her tongue too, shy and hesitant at first, but then bolder and with confidence.

He rubbed her around a little more, and managed to sneak in a little more than just the kissing.

Not that he grabbed her. Lord, no. She would've whacked him if he'd done a thing like that, he was sure.

But he did let the side of his wrist kind

of ride up against where he oughtn't to have been.

He really did grow faint with excitement when that happened, and he quickly pulled his hand back lest it become obvious what he was doing and Sarah get mad.

But, oh, goodness, that was some fine hayride, this last one he expected ever to take. Goodness gracious indeed.

33

It was one, two o'clock in the morning by the time they got back to town. It looked like half the community had come out to meet them despite the late hour, parents collecting their kids and like that. Every year it seemed pretty much the whole town lost sleep the night of the hayride.

Mr. Young, unfortunately, was there to escort Sarah home, and some of the other girls with her. Johnny had to pretend like nothing happened on the hayride. Not that so awful much did. But it was hard standing there with Sarah's dad there too. Not after the things the two of them had been doing just a minute or two ago.

Johnny wanted to take her in his arms again and give her a proper good-bye. Good-bye? What he really wanted was to take her off someplace where there weren't any other folks and do even more than they'd done on the way back to town.

What did happen was that he stood there like a big dumb lump while Sarah gave him a nod and extended her hand for him to shake. A handshake, for crying out loud. A lousy handshake. Grab her and hold her and lick her tonsils, that would have been more like it.

Instead he just nodded, looking as solemn and ordinary as she did, and lightly touched her fingertips in the sort of handshake that was appropriate between a boy and a girl who had no announced intentions.

The little kids got picked up and carried home on their parents' shoulders. The middling-aged boys went whooping and bouncing off toward their own homes. The girls of middle size and bigger got escorted home in the night. And Johnny and Andy and Pipper — Johnny hadn't seen who, if anybody, Pipper rode back with — climbed back onto the wagon to ride with Mr. Hemple over to the livery so they could help him with the harness and collect their ponies from his corral. Tomorrow after church they would help him unload and pitch the hay into the loft for him.

It was about all Johnny could do to keep from floating clean off the wagon. He was feeling that good. Dreamy, like.

While they helped out at the livery and then for a little while after, leaning on the corral rail and sort of rehashing the evening, Andy got to telling everything he'd done in the hay with old Becky, and it turned out Pipper had done some necking too, with freckle-faced and chunky Gretchen Swanson.

"You should've seen her poor little sister, Johnny. Janie kept looking for you, trying to figure out where you were and who you was with. Gretchen said she has an awful crush on you, y'know. Janie, I mean, not Gretchen. She said Janie wanted to get snug and cuddly with you, never mind that she's only twelve. I don't think she ever did figure it out where you were." Pipper paused. "Where, uh, where was you anyway? Who was you with?"

Johnny just smiled. Pipper and Andy could brag all they wanted. What they'd been doing tonight was just play. They didn't have any serious feelings toward Becky or Gretchen.

Johnny now, his feelings were plumb serious.

And he didn't say word one about that or about the kissing and the touching that'd gone on underneath Sarah's cloak. No, sir. Not a single word.

34

There are plenty of things a cattleman has to worry about, but finding something to do is not one of them. In summer there are screwworms to fight and mud bogs to drag cattle out of. In fall there is the gathering and culling and driving to market. In winter the problem is water holes iced over and fallen cattle with broken legs. In springtime it is the calving and later the branding and earmarking. Always there is something. But if any season could be said to be slack, it would be that brief period between marketing the year's crop and the onset of hard winter. That was the time of year Johnny liked best.

Oh, there was still more than enough work to do. He and his father still had to keep an eye on their herd, looking for injuries or diseases or whatever else might befall the amazingly stupid bovine creatures, and at home it was the time of year when time was available for the inevitable repairs needed. Gates, fences, hinges, saddles, and harnesses, sometimes it seemed every article and item was as busy at the tasks of self-destruction as the Ackermans were at maintaining them.

They were still busy at this time of year then, but the pace of the work was slower.

"This look like a good spot?" his father asked, kneeing his old gelding toward a brushy depression that if nothing else would get them out of the chill, incessant wind.

"Whatever you say."

"We'll stop here for our nooning then," Lewis Ackerman said. "Since you're so all-fired enthusiastic."

"Yessir."

"Don't go building a fire, though. Too much wind right now and everything's too dry. I expect we can get along without coffee for one meal. Does that sound good to you?" Lewis waited, turned around in his saddle, and repeated, "Does that sound good to you?"

"What does?" Johnny asked.

"What I just said."

"I, uh . . ."

"You didn't hear a word I said, did you?"

"Sure I did."

161

His father smiled. "I believe you, son. So what was it that I just said?"

"I, um, I may've missed a word or two."

"Follow me, son. And when we step down, don't go building any fire. We aren't gonna make coffee now."

"Whatever you say."

They hobbled the horses and pulled their saddles so the animals could roll if they wanted without breaking anything. Johnny dragged out the bundle that held the lunch his mother packed for them that morning, and automatically began casting about for the makings of a small fire.

"Johnny."

"Yes?"

"What did I tell you about a fire today?"

"Oh, right. I guess I forgot."

"Yes, I guess you did. It's something you seem to be doing a lot of these days."

"I'm sorry. Have I done something wrong?"

"No, you haven't. That isn't what I was getting at. Hand me that canteen, will you? Thanks. Now sit down over here and let's see what your mama put in our poke today, shall we?"

Ten or fifteen minutes later, Lewis dragged out his pipe and lighted it — concern about fire could be overdone — and gave Johnny a slow looking over while he got the pipe to draw properly. "Something is bothering you, son. What is it?"

"Nothing. Really."

"All right. It isn't bothering you. But it's damn sure got all your attention of late. Or the biggest piece of it anyhow. If you want to talk about it, whatever it is, I'm here. You know what I'm saying?"

"Yes, sir. Thank you."

"But there isn't anything you want to tell me? Or ask?"

"No, not really."

"That's fine. Whenever you're ready."

"Yes, sir."

Lewis lay back, propping his neck against the age-slick seat of his saddle and drawing contentedly on the pipe while he watched a pair of thin clouds drift slowly overhead.

"Pop."

"Yes, son?"

"When you left home, left Grampa, I mean, and went out on your own, how did you go about making a start for yourself?"

"You surprise me, John. I didn't expect we'd be having this discussion for another five or ten years yet."

"Is it all right? I'm not making you mad or anything, am I?"

Lewis smiled. "No, son. You're just fine." He pursed his lips and closed his eyes in thought for a moment. "I don't really know how to go about telling you all the things you want to know. But I'll sure give 'er a try. I'd guess I was, oh, twenty-four or thereabouts when I got to thinking it was time for me to set out." He chuckled softly. "I'd just met your mama then, do you see, and the truth is, that's what got me to thinking about it. So what I did was . . ."

If any of the cattle were in trouble that afternoon, they were just going to have to work it out on their own, at least until tomorrow. It was nearly dark and the temperatures were plummeting before Johnny and his dad saddled their horses and set off for home.

35

"Goodness, dear, you're in an awfully good humor this morning," his mom said as Johnny bustled around helping to get things ready for the drive to church. He'd gotten his chores done before daybreak, then hurried inside to help prepare the picnic basket.

His father sat at the table smiling just a little and smoking his pipe. His dad hadn't exactly been told who was at the bottom of this excitement, but it was no trick for him to make a guess. And that particular party hadn't been at services last week following the late-night hayride. "Son."

"Yes, Pop?"

"Time to get 'em hitched up."

Johnny bobbed his head and grabbed his sheepskin coat off a peg beside the door. He bolted out practically at a run.

"Whatever has gotten into him?" Stella Ackerman asked with a shake of her head.

Lewis grinned. "Spring fever."

"Silly. It's only fall."

"I'm not talking about the weather."

"And what do you mean by that, may I ask?"

"Just what I said," Lewis told her from behind a cloud of aromatic smoke.

Stella sniffed loudly and turned back to packing away greasy chunks of the cold bacon she'd cooked the night before. "Men!" she retorted aloud.

"Exactly," her husband said in a soft voice that she may not even have heard.

36

Johnny was in such an excellent mood that he didn't even mind when Sarah sang with that fancy boy from back East. She and Foster and Catherine Becker sang a — it took him a moment to remember it was called a trio when there were three of them — sang "Bringing in the Sheaves." As a trio. Three of them. He sat on the bench smiling and nodding his approval and enjoying this probably more than any Sunday service he could remember. Ever.

For a change Mr. Tolliver's preaching even sounded pretty good to him, although later he couldn't have told anybody what the sermon was about. Not to save his soul. Which his mother would have said it was. During the preaching part of the service, Johnny just sat back with his arms folded and enjoyed looking at Sarah's pretty face. He surely did like the soft look of her skin and the way a wisp of stray hair curled onto that softness in front of her ear.

What he liked even more than the look of her cheek was the memory of what it felt like. What it tasted like. What . . .

Johnny began to squirm on the hard bench. He was becoming all worked up again, and if Mr. Tolliver came to an early end of his message and they all had to stand up to sing the next hymn, well, that would be awful damned embarrassing. Fortunately, worrying about the bulge in his britches made the problem go away. But he kept on looking at Sarah. And the same dang problem kept coming back and then going away again when he thought about that more than he was thinking about her.

For about ten or twenty minutes there he was plenty uncomfortable, though, and in a way he was glad when the sermon did end so that his mind wasn't wandering quite so much.

The congregation sang the last hymn and Mr. Tolliver gave a benediction. Mr. Tolliver always looked uncomfortable when he did that, like as if he didn't figure it was right for a blacksmith to be handing out blessings the way a real preacher would, one who'd been to preaching school and got consecrated or whatever the heck it was that they did to make them preachers.

Soon as the last words of the benediction were spoken, the place erupted with the thunder of hard shoes on the wooden floor as the little kids and the almost-little ones went racing for the door.

The older folks knew to hang back and give the young ones time to bundle up and get clear of the vestibule before anybody else tried to get in there to where the coats were.

The choir went around behind a muslin-covered screen to exchange their robes for their coats. They would come out the back and meet everyone outside.

Johnny suspected this might be the last Sunday with temperatures mild enough that they could eat outdoors. Come the hard cold or snow, or the rain in milder times, they all had to crowd together indoors to eat, and when that happened there was no privacy during the whole of the afternoon. He was pleased they would be outside today.

And he wondered if it would be too soon to ask Sarah to come eat with him and his folks. To sort of make it clear to the town who she was with and what John

Harold Ackerman's intentions were.

He was trembling more than a little when he finally was able to get into the vestibule and grab his coat and hat.

37

"I can't, Johnny. I promised Mama I'd get together with her and Mrs. Ballew this afternoon and go over the Sunday School lessons." Sarah smiled and rather proudly added, "I'm going to teach the six- and seven-year-olds for the next quarter."

"I didn't know," he said lamely.

Sarah's smile remained. "I talked to Mr. Tolliver about it weeks and weeks ago. I think it'll be fun. And good practice."

"Practice?"

"That's something else that I bet you don't know. As soon as I turn sixteen I'm going to take the examination for a teaching certificate. I want to be a teacher, you see."

"You do?"

She bobbed her head ever so sweetly, her dimples showing and her eyes sparkling bright. He'd never seen anything so pretty. Not ever.

Did she know . . . did she care . . . that her words were driving stakes into his heart?

If Sarah got herself a job as a teacher, it wasn't likely to be anywhere around here. Redhorse Butte already had a teacher. A smart-aleck annoying damned fancy-boy teacher, but anyway a teacher. If Sarah was serious about this teaching stuff, she would have to go someplace else to do it.

And teachers aren't allowed to be married or even step out with boyfriends. Teachers have to be about as circumspect and fuddy-duddy as preachers. Maybe even more so.

Johnny's mood was pretty sour over lunch, which he had to eat with Andy and Pipper instead of with Sarah like he'd hoped.

He got to feeling better about it all later on during the second go-round of preaching, for then it occurred to him that maybe if Sarah got herself licensed to teach, *she* could teach all the kids here at Redhorse Butte and Ed Foster could go someplace else to annoy the good folks.

There were, in fact, several places that Johnny thought would be just about right for Foster. Hell came to mind right off. Or anyway Purgatory.

Not that he really had any reason to dislike the fancy boy.

He found himself smiling.

Not after the hayride, he needn't worry about the dang schoolmaster.

He sat there feeling considerably better after that, and even managed to pay some attention to Mr. Tolliver's afternoon sermon.

38

Johnny slid the handle of his ax through the loop he'd tied in his saddle strings and let the ax dangle there out of the way. He stepped back onto the ugly brindle-colored horse, and paused for a moment to catch his breath and to wipe his brow with the back of his gloved hand.

He was sorely tempted to take his gloves off and open the front of his coat to some fresh air, but he knew he dasn't do it.

Johnny never ceased to be surprised at how hot and sweaty a person could get when the temperatures were so cheek-numbing cold. You had to be bundled up to the eyeballs in order to keep from freezing half to death when you were riding, but then once you got to doing heavy work, inside all that clothing you began to sweat.

And then the danger was that when you quit the exertion you'd get cold again, the cold air drying the sweat but reaching deep inside because of the wetness. That right there was what brought on the pneumonia, and as young as he was, Johnny had already seen a neighbor and good friend of his folks die of the pneumonia after he worked up a sweat splitting stove lengths and made the mistake of taking his coat off afterward.

MacEuen would have been all right, everyone said, if he'd left his coat on or if he went inside right away, but he hadn't. He'd worked up a good sweat splitting the wood chunks, took his coat off, and then stayed outside to stack the wood he'd just finished splitting.

That was two years ago. MacEuen hadn't lasted out the month before his lungs filled up and he died trying to draw breath.

Of course MacEuen had been old already. Well into his forties, his widow said. She was a younger woman, MacEuen's second wife. She'd packed up and left to go back to her own folks someplace back East. Johnny heard, but didn't know for sure, that she'd left the two children, both of them by MacEuen's first wife, at an orphanage someplace.

Of course if anything like that were to

happen to him, the only people who'd be discommoded would be his mom and pop. And Sarah Young. Maybe.

Johnny reined his horse away from the water hole he'd just finished chopping open, and headed across the ridge toward the next watering place.

He rode with his head tucked deep inside the muffler his mother always forced him to wear — and which he appreciated even if he did fuss about it every time — and idly wondered what Sarah would do if he did up and die young, before the two of them married or announced themselves or so much as did anything. Of an intimate nature, that is. Which they hadn't. Yet.

Usually thinking about that possibility was enough to get him powerfully worked up, but this morning he let it slide on by while his thoughts speculated about his own death and how folks would react to it if it happened.

Andy and Pipper and maybe a couple of the other fellows would miss him. He was sure of that.

But Sarah.

Would she fall to pieces, weeping and blubbering and her nose running snot? Would she grieve in dignified silence? Or declare that she would become a spinster schoolteacher and eschew — that was a good word, eschew; he kind of liked it but couldn't remember ever actually using it in a sentence out loud — any other love forevermore?

Would she get over him someday? Even forget him soon? Right away?

Johnny wondered about that, and kind of wished he could find out. The trick to that, of course, was making this discovery without having to actually die in order to do so.

The fact of it was that this was something he would never really know. Not for sure. Not even if he and Sarah got married and lived together for the next fifty years.

The horse found its way down the hillside and across a wide, bare flat covered with stem-cured brown grasses, and on to the next water. It had turned almighty cold now on the cusp between autumn and winter, so they had to worry about keeping the water holes open, but there hadn't yet been any snow to speak of, just a little dusting now and then, and that wasn't enough to worry about. The cattle could find all the graze they wanted when it was like this, and the cold never seemed to bother them in the least. So long as Johnny and his pop kept the ice chopped so the critters could drink, they would be just fine.

Johnny pulled up and took a moment to get his breath and put his thoughts back onto business, then stepped down off the brindle and pulled the ax out of the keeper.

He eyed the horse, thinking about leaving it ground-tied for the few minutes this would take him. Then he thought about how dang far he'd have to walk if the horse decided to go home without him.

Better safe than sorry, his pop always said. That sounded like pretty good advice in a situation like this, so he dropped the ax onto the frozen turf and took the time to hobble the horse before he retrieved the ax and went down to the watering point.

39

"What day did you say it is?" Johnny asked.

"Saturday a week. Not this coming Saturday, mind, but a week from it," Pipper told him.

Johnny grinned. The annual Christmas dance was one of the major events in Redhorse Butte. Bigger than the hayride. Almost as big as Fourth of July. Which was the biggest thing there was, what with all the county officials — the ones looking to be reelected anyway — coming to make speeches and proclaim proclamations and that stuff while the folks had wrestling matches and horseraces and footraces and ate a whole steer that one of the fellows would donate every year, doing that turn and turn about so no one person got stuck losing a beef too often. Last year the Ackermans gave the steer, then the men-folk in pretty much the whole community came out to tend the coals and turn the spit the day before and all through that night. It was quite an occasion, the Fourth of July.

This dance wouldn't be quite that much fun, but it was always good.

Unlike a regular dance, for Christmas everybody showed up early and shared a meal and drank cider — not all of it soft, though the women pretended not to know that — and wore their Sunday best.

Mr. Truax and the other musicians opened their playing with some slow stuff, waltzes and like that, though they weren't much good at that sort of thing. They did it, though, so the older folks could get in some dancing before the boot-stomping crowd got down to the square dancing.

"Will you be helping us clear out the barn?" Pipper asked.

"You know I will."

"Come in first thing in the morning then. Me and the rest of the boys will meet you at Hemple's. Then when we're done, maybe we can do a little shopping. Getting ready for the dance, if you know what I mean."

"Just make sure you don't try an' save money this time. It's coming Christmas for crying out loud. Get the good stuff, will you?" Johnny teased. And with good reason. For the last dance, that darn Pipper brought a big bottle of the awfulest-tasting Injun whiskey Johnny ever heard tell of. It was so awful they'd had to cut it three to one with sweetened fruit punch just so they could stand to drink it.

Which was not to say that anybody refused to drink it, of course. It was the only whiskey they had. But they weren't going to let Pipper forget that. Not hardly.

"All right then. Saturday a week."

"D'you want to slip over to Henley's and have a little something now?" Otis Henley owned Redhorse Butte's only saloon. It was really as much a hog ranch as a saloon, for a man could find all manner of sinfulness there. Henley did most of his business after dark so his customers wouldn't be easily seen coming and going. Everybody knew who patronized the place in spite of that, of course. But it was considered proper to make the effort for the sake of appearances.

"Or we could ride up to Conyer and have us a blowout if you'd rather." Conyer was the only other town in the basin. The young bucks and old bachelors — and bachelors-for-a-night — from Conyer came down to Redhorse Butte whenever they wanted to raise serious Cain, and the fellows from Redhorse Butte went to Conyer when they had those same impulses.

Johnny shook his head. "Not today, thanks. There's some other stuff I need to do here in town, and I don't want beer on my breath when I do it."

Pipper raised an eyebrow. Then he figured it out and began to grin. "Next time," he said.

"Next time," Johnny agreed with a laugh.

"I hear the thunder of little feet, so I reckon school's out for the day an' you can get on with your town business," Pipper said.

"See you later, pard." Johnny began buttoning his coat while he headed out of Archer's in search of his date — he hoped — for the big dance.

40

"I'm sorry, Johnny. Sarah isn't here," Mrs. Young told him. "Would you like to come inside and wait for her? She shouldn't be long."

"Oh, no, ma'am, thank you." Johnny always felt uncomfortable around Sarah's folks. Probably because of what he hoped to do to their daughter the very first chance he got. Except that wasn't quite right. It was what he wanted to do *with* Sarah, not *to* her. He sure did want to do it, though.

"You might look for her at the mercantile then. She sometimes stops in there with her girlfriends."

"I just came from there," Johnny said.

Mrs. Young smiled bright as a new penny. Sarah got her smile from her mom, there was no doubt about that. "Then I suggest you look in the school. That nice Mr. Foster has been tutoring her, getting

her ready for the teaching examination."
Mrs. Young's smile became even brighter.
"I wouldn't mention that except Sarah told
me she's already told you what she hopes
to do next summer."

"Yes, ma'am, she did. I'll take a look in
there. Thank you."

"My pleasure, son."

Johnny stepped back from the door and
rather gratefully put his hat on. His head
was getting cold without it.

"Oh, Johnny."

"Yes'm?"

"When you see Sarah, remind her to
stop at the store and pick up a pint of
leather britches, will you please?"

"Yes, ma'am." Once he was off the porch
Johnny made a face, glad he wasn't going
to be eating with the Youngs tonight. He
didn't like the dried green beans. Lucky for
him his father didn't like them either, so
his mom gave up cooking them ages ago.
Nowadays, the only times he had to suffer
through them was at church socials or like
that when others brought them.

His step quickened, not only from the
cold either, as he headed toward the
schoolhouse.

41

The schoolhouse wasn't but a few hundred yards from the Youngs' place, but Johnny was chilled to the bone by the time he got there. It was going to be a very cold ride home this evening.

But then he would have his thoughts about Sarah to keep him warm on the way. Keep him from sleeping afterward too probably.

Johnny stepped into the vestibule, feeling the warmth immediately . . . and gratefully. He stripped off his gloves and started unbuttoning his coat as he entered the single large room that served the needs of the children of all ages, the youngest seated closest to the front and the older kids toward the rear. There were three different-sized desks, the smallest toward the front and the largest at the back of the room.

There were only two people in the place at this hour, the fancy boy and Sarah.

They huddled together at the very front of the room. Sarah had pulled a chair over to the teacher's big desk. She and Foster sat there side by side, both of them leaning down over something on the desk surface with their heads almost touching.

They must not have heard Johnny come in. Both of them jumped as if startled, and sat bolt upright when he stamped his feet to knock the snow off his boots so he wouldn't track it onto the floor beyond the vestibule. The vestibule floor was already muddy from the comings and goings of the children.

"Johnny! Did you just now get here?" Sarah asked, the fingers of one delicate hand pressed to her chest.

"Uh-huh. Your mom said I could prob'ly find you here."

"Yes, Ed . . . Mr. Foster, that is . . . is helping me study. For the exam. You know."

"Sure." Johnny looked at Foster and silently gave the schoolmaster a nod. There was no reason for him to be jealous of the fancy boy. He knew that now. But he still didn't particularly like the SOB.

Foster gave the gesture scant acknowledgment, moving his head just enough to suggest a nod.

"I wanted to talk t' you about some-thing," Johnny said.

"It's all right," Foster said softly, his voice carrying in the empty room. "We should quit for the day now anyway. It will be dark soon, and I still have to clean up and prepare the stove for tomorrow."

"I was going to mop the floor for you," Sarah told him.

"Thank you, but I can manage. Go along with your little friend now."

Johnny felt his blood commence to boil. "Little friend," was it? All the hostility he'd felt before came rushing back. And an-other big helping to go along with it. Arro-gant damned Easterner!

Sarah sighed and closed the large book that the two of them had been bent so close above. She stood and said something to Foster in a voice too low for Johnny to hear. Then she put a smile onto her face and came to the back of the room to meet him.

Johnny fetched her cloak — he had fond memories of that cloak — off the peg and held it for her, then buttoned his coat shut again and held the door for her.

"We need to go over to Archer's," he said. "Your mom needs some stuff." He made a face. "Leather britches. Ugh." The frown turned into a smile. "And I want to talk to you about the Christmas dance. I'd sure like to squire you to it."

She touched his elbow. "Oh, Johnny. I'd love for you to, but I'm on the refreshment committee. Becky and I are going to help decorate and make the punch. I already promised."

"Then will you at least save some dances for me?" He reached for her and leaned down to give her a little kiss, but she ducked away, smiling. "Not here in broad daylight," she cautioned, although she didn't sound angry. "Tongues would wag, you know."

"I wouldn't care if they did," he protested.

"Well, I would. Now be good or you won't get any hugging and kissing at the dance either."

Johnny grumbled a little, but not too seriously. Girls worried about stuff like that, he knew. God knows why. It was only a little kiss he wanted. For now.

"You can walk me home from the store if you want," Sarah suggested. Half a heartbeat later she smiled and reminded him, "No one can see inside the vestibule, you know. And my mother won't come rushing even if she does hear us come inside. We ought to have a minute or two of privacy there." The smile became impish. "If you want to, that is."

If he wanted to? *If* he wanted? Oh, my.

"I expect I can stand it if you can," he said, trying to sound like it didn't matter. Not even a little bit.

Sarah laughed and squeezed his elbow.

By then they were on the broad street and really would be seen if he tried anything. He helped her step up onto the sidewalk boards and rushed ahead to open the mercantile door for her.

42

Johnny was light-headed when he finally started for home. He only left then because Mrs. Young came out to see what was taking Sarah so long to bring the dang leather britches inside.

It had been kind of embarrassing standing there looking Sarah's mom in the face after . . . well, it wasn't like he'd done anything all that serious standing in the chilly vestibule. But this evening he had the taste of Sarah's lips in his mouth and the feel of her flesh burned into his hand too. Not as much as he wanted to feel. But more than he'd ever expected.

He'd touched her, just a little, putting his hand underneath her cloak, feeling the warmth that seeped through the cloth of her school dress and through whatever it was that girls wore underneath that outer garment. He knew girls wore stuff in layers. He'd felt it. He had no knowledge of what-all was under there.

Well, in truth maybe he did have *some* idea. About the possibilities of what grown-up women wore under their dresses, if not the reality of what Sarah in particular was wearing today.

After all, when he looked through the Montgomery Ward catalog, it wasn't only the boots and the tools and stuff that he looked at on those pages.

When he'd been younger, he'd gone as far as to very carefully tear those pages out of the outdated catalogs that were being discarded — he'd have died from mortal embarrassment if his mother ever saw that he'd snitched pages . . . and which ones — then fold them real careful and hide them to come back to time and time again so as to fantasize about what those mysterious items might cover.

Andy and Pipper had done the same. He knew that, for they'd giggled and talked about it sometimes. Even compared pages, opinions, and naughty speculations now and then. Now that they were grown, they likely would laugh about such juvenile practices if the subject ever came up.

But if anything, Johnny's interest in those mysteries was even more feverish today than it was when they were twelve or fourteen or like that.

He shivered — from his train of thought and not the cold — and crawled onto his saddle.

His eyes got wide and he sat bolt upright for a moment there before he forced himself to relax onto the seat. He was sure enough wide awake and paying attention to business now, though, after encountering the cold leather. Sitting down on that saddle now was like straddling a block of ice. Got his attention, that was for sure.

There were times, like right now, when he thought maybe there was something to be said for riding inside a covered and buttoned-up rig, a hansom or an opera coach or that sort of thing, where you could bury yourself nose-deep in lap robes and shawls and maybe set a charcoal brazier on the floor to keep your feet warm.

Sitting here on this dang horse now was about as cold as Johnny ever hoped to get.

He touched a heel to the ugly old thing's side and bumped it up into a canter that he hoped would get the blood to moving and warm them both, for it was going to be a long ride home tonight.

43

"What in the world are you doing?"

Johnny looked up and grinned. "Oh, hi, Pop. I just thought . . . what with the snow and all . . ."

The dry cold had ended. With something of a vengeance. It had been snowing for two nights and a day and was still coming down, the big, soft, heavy wet flakes like you sometimes got early in the winter or at the tag end of it. There was probably a foot and a half of the stuff lying clean and pretty over everything.

Perhaps because of the snow or the clouds it fell from, the temperatures were not so biting cold as they had been. And of course, having a good snowfall meant there would be moisture in the ground come spring to encourage the grass to grow.

Johnny was busy working inside the barn. He had the right side of the wagon jacked up and propped on chunks of unsplit firewood. The front wheel was off, and he was busy removing the rear one. A steel sled runner was laid on the floor on each side of the wagon ready to be bolted on in place of the wheels.

"You wouldn't want to be borrowing the wagon for tomorrow, would you?"

The grin became wider. "I thought maybe. If you and Mama don't mind. You, uh, won't be using it, will you?"

"No, we aren't going to the dance this year."

"So can I? Use the wagon, I mean?"

His father smiled and nodded. Then he laughed and said, "Remember to throw in a couple blankets and the buffalo robe. You might toss some hay into the back too. But don't mention that to your mother. I don't know that she would be so happy to know what her baby is up to."

"Pop!"

"Well . . . you know."

Johnny grinned again.

"You be careful, though, you hear? Go too far and there could be consequences. If you know what I mean."

"Pop, really. It isn't anything like that. Honest."

His father harrumphed, then cleared his throat and spit. "If it isn't, then it will be because she won't let you. Remember, I used to be your age. I know how I was, and I think your generation is even worse than mine was."

Johnny rolled his eyes. But he didn't bother denying anything. Besides, his father hadn't come right out and suggested anything specific for Johnny *to* deny. That made it difficult to plead his innocence.

"D'you think you'll need some help getting those mounts to line up? Those runners are a bitch to put on when they get to flexing. Easier if there's two doing the job."

"I don't want to put you out."

"I don't mind. Now finish with that wheel, and we'll bolt 'er snug and get the other side tended to."

"Thanks, Pop. You, uh, you're all right. I mean . . . I don't tell you that as much as I should, I suppose. But it's the truth. You're okay."

Lewis Ackerman took hold of Johnny's shoulder and gave it a squeeze. "You aren't so bad your own self." He winked and added, "Some of the time."

Johnny lifted the back wheel off, and his father took hold of the spindly, flexible sled runner and dragged it in place for them to work on.

44

" 'Tisn't fair," Andy complained.

"What isn't?"

Andy nodded toward the big doors at the front of the barn where Becky and Sarah and a handful of the other girls were dragging in greenery and bunting and such by the basket- and armload.

"So?"

"So they're dressed in their old clothes. They can go home and change before the dance. Get all fancied up and pretty. We got to be careful of our riggin's and we'll still wind up all covered with horse shit."

Pipper threw a handful of straw at him. "What difference does it make to the likes of you? You won't be getting near any of those sweet things anyway."

"Well, you never know. Could be that I might . . . if I didn't come to these dances smelling like a mule's hind end after we clean the place and get it all ready."

"Your problem, Andy, is that you *look* like a mule's hind end. They none of them ever come close enough to you t' find out what you smell like," Johnny said.

Andy grinned. "I hadn't thought about that. Could be you're right."

"Now lookahere," Pipper said, "we're done here, right? And if we hang around, those girls are just gonna rope us into doing the decorating while they stand around giving orders. I say we go find us a place where we can keep warm and maybe have a nip or two t' keep the chill off."

"I could sure stand to warm up, now that's a fact." Johnny wrapped his arms tight over his chest and shivered. "I wisht Mr. Hemple would let us drag a couple stoves in here. It's gonna be awful cold in here tonight, even with a bunch of folks crowding in."

"Aw, it's cold every year for the Christmas dance."

"And I don't blame Mr. Hemple for not wanting to risk allowing a fire. It's too dangerous."

"Sure is cold, though."

"Get a couple drinks in you and stomp around the floor a few times and you won't feel so cold."

"My pop says drinking and courting

don't mix. Well, not unless it's the girl that's doing the drinking."

"Your pop never said no such thing. I don't believe that for a minute, no, sir."

"He would have said it if he'd thought about it, though."

"So are we gonna stand here freezing our ears off. . . ."

"Or other parts."

"Hush, will you? I'm talking here."

"Yes, sir. Sorry, sir. My apologies, sir."

"Like I was saying . . . let's go find something to warm us up."

"You're the one standing around talking about it. Us two are just waitin' for you to hush up so we can go."

Laughing, the three put away the tools they'd been using to clean out the livery stable, then stepped outside.

Johnny paused for a moment at the door. Even bundled to her ears and wearing a ratty old linen duster over top of a coat and her regular clothes, Sarah looked prettier than a new pup.

He was feeling pretty darn good, and that was the truth.

45

"Are you okay?"

"I'm fine," Johnny said. "Really." He weaved just a little and grabbed hold of Pipper's shoulder for a little assistance with his balance.

Inside the noisy, crowded, happy barn full of folks, Johnny felt a little too warm. Almost hot. But he must be cold, he thought, because his cheeks were numb. And he couldn't feel the tip of his nose. That seemed odd, because he hadn't thought it was that cold.

Not that it mattered. The Christmas party was a nice one. Mr. Truax and his band — well, sort of a band, as close to being a band as they could muster in Redhorse Butte — they were sawing away at their instruments and the folks were dancing to Mr. Hemple's call.

The decorations made the big old livery stable downright festive. The girls had found some juniper branches to provide greenery, and they and the smaller kids had made stars and bows and such using old newspapers dyed different bright colors and glued into the desired shapes with flour paste. Paper chains were hung all over, and there were ropes of popcorn strung on thread. Those wouldn't last too long, for the little kids kept eating them, stealing the puffy kernels and giggling fit to bust when they got away with it. Which they always did because after all, what's the point of having a popcorn string if some kid can't eat it?

It occurred to Johnny that they hadn't gotten around to having any supper. They'd had a little whiskey. A little beer. But he hadn't eaten since . . . he scowled as he tried to think . . . breakfast, that was it. He hadn't eaten any actual food since breakfast.

Not that he minded. He was feeling just fine. Except for being just the least bit numb, that is.

But he was all right. Really.

He looked across the room to where the girls were. Sarah was wearing a white dress with red and green snowflakes embroidered on the . . . whatever you called that part of a dang dress. On the chest part is what it was.

The top of it was cut daringly low. Low enough that Johnny couldn't hardly quit looking.

And there was a ring of ruffledy puffs at the sleeves and along the bottom. Hem? He thought that was what the bottom part was. Thought that was what his mother called it.

Not that it made any difference. The point was that Sarah looked like an angel. A real, genuine, sure enough angel come to life right here in Montana. And wasn't that something.

Looking at her was enough to make a fellow just right up and love her.

Love! There. He'd thought the very word. Wasn't ready to say it out loud just yet. But until now he hadn't even wanted to form it in his head. It's a scary word, love. Pretty. But mighty heavy.

Johnny took a deep, deep breath and thought about marching right straight across the stable floor and asking Sarah to dance.

He was going to do it too. This time, for the first time, he was going to do it.

After all, she'd kissed all over him on the hayride, hadn't she? So why the heck wouldn't she want to dance with him now?

Of course, nobody else had been

watching when they were in the back of the hay wagon, and it was at night. This was with the lanterns bright and practically the whole community inside the barn.

Oh, gosh. The hay wagon was parked right out back of this building. There was hay in it too. Johnny was sure of that because him and Andy unloaded part of Mr. Hemple's hay and tossed it up to the loft so Pipper could arrange it up there for the little kids to crawl into and go to sleep when the dance went into the small hours, as it certainly would. It always did, year after year.

Johnny thought about Sarah. And about that hay. And he knew just exactly where he wanted to take her when he went to squire her home from the dance.

Come to think of it, he realized, he hadn't yet asked her about driving her home.

He hoped her folks didn't mind if he did that. They were here at the dance too, skipping and bowing and allemande this or allemande that along with the rest of the crowd. They might want to take her home with them. Lordy, he hoped not.

What he figured was that he'd wait until her folks left before he asked Sarah about stepping out into the dark with him. He could try to get her alone now, but then her folks might decide to go home early, and get mad when they found that Sarah and Johnny'd left the dance, like, an hour earlier and still weren't to the house. Oh, wouldn't that be a disgrace and a scandal.

No, better for him to let them leave first. Then he could take Sarah outside and around to the hay wagon and burrow down deep inside the hay, and her folks would think she was still at the dance hopping around where the whole town could keep an eye on things.

He liked that. He surely did.

But he was going to have to ask her. Maybe dance with her too.

Damn fancy boy from back East wasn't shy about dancing. While Johnny stood there watching, that damn schoolmaster Foster stopped in front of Sarah and bowed to her and held out his elbow, holding it stiff and cocked like he was a chicken with a busted wing.

Fancy SOB. He was dressed to the nines. Flouncy-puffy yellow silk thing at his throat — all the better to throttle him with was Johnny's opinion — and a tailor-sewed suit of charcoal-colored clothes and bright polished shoes with yellow canvas ankle-protector things. Spats were those called?

Silly-looking damn things anyway. And a yellow silk waistband thing where a belt ought to be.

Foster was no threat to him. Johnny knew that. But he still didn't like the son of a bitch. Just couldn't help it. There was something about Ed Foster that just plain grated on Johnny's nerves.

Johnny took a deep breath and squared his shoulders and prepared himself for the ordeal of walking across the room with all the folks watching and asking Sarah to step out onto the dance floor with him.

He was going to do that. Do it right now too. He really was.

He took one more deep breath and a step forward.

And saw that damned Foster smile and hold his hand out.

Saw Sarah flash her dimples and place her fingertips onto the back of Foster's hand. She dipped into a curtsey, and Foster bowed to her. Bowed real low and proper he did, the son of a bitch.

Then he led Sarah out and tossed his head back and launched into the reel they happened to be playing at the moment.

Damn him!

And Sarah. She didn't have to act like she was enjoying herself so much, did she?

Johnny frowned and turned his back on the dance floor. Where'd that damn Pipper get to? Pipper had the best part of a pint hidden under his coat. He'd have just one more sip. Then he'd go out onto the floor and tap Mr. Back-Damn-East on the shoulder to cut in on him.

That, he decided, was exactly what he would do.

Just as soon as he found Pipper and the pint bottle.

46

"No!"

Johnny blinked.

"You are drunk, Johnny Ackerman. You can't hardly walk and you can't hardly talk and you reek of demon alcohol and no, I will *not* step outside with you."

Johnny blinked again. He could not believe it. His girl, his very own girlfriend, wouldn't go outside to spark and spoon. He opened his mouth to protest, but belched instead. The belch tasted pretty dang bad too. He frowned and thought about how it would taste if someone was to kiss him when he had breath that bad.

And that somehow struck him as funny. He began to laugh.

The laughing kept him from getting mad, and after a moment the laughing kind of tailed off into a few chuckles and then he managed to get control of himself. He tried again.

"Sa . . . Sarah. I brung . . . brought . . . blanket. Out inna wagon. You know? Wanna hug anna kiss. You know?" He giggled.

He was in a good mood, deliberately forgetting the fact that she'd turned him down on the pretext that he might've had just the least little bit too much to drink. Which of course he had not. He was just fine. Really.

He grinned and laughed a little more and reached out to touch Sarah's shoulder. His balance was not everything it might have been and he stumbled. The hand that was intended to lightly touch her shoulder darted lower as he lurched forward, and by accident he pawed the front of Sarah's party dress. Right below the red and green snowflakes. Right on top of her right breast.

Sarah yelped and jumped back.

Ed Foster, the son of a bitch, stepped in and with a cold-faced snarl batted Johnny's arm down.

Johnny peered at the schoolmaster in disbelief. Then regaining his wits — how dare Foster think he could do that and get away with it — hauled off and socked the schoolteacher one.

"You assaulted me!" Foster declared.

There was a red patch, sort of like a blush, on Foster's cheek, but he seemed otherwise undamaged.

"Yeah, an' I gonna do it 'gain too. Gonna whup your ass, fancy boy. Gonna . . . gonna . . . gonna whup you." Johnny pulled his fist back and launched it a second time.

Foster swayed to the side and Johnny's punch sailed harmlessly wide. Dang schoolteacher was lucky that time. Johnny belched and swayed on his feet and blinked a little. "Gonna whup you, boy."

"Stop it, will you?" Foster barked. "You are making a spectacle of yourself. Now stop bothering people. Go sleep it off somewhere."

"Gonna . . . gonna whup you." Johnny tried to step around Foster so he could take Sarah by the hand and lead her outside. He had to explain, after all. Had to make sure she knew he hadn't intended to grab her there. Besides, he still wanted that hugging and kissing he'd been looking forward to all this time.

"Stop, Ackerman," Foster ordered. "I'll not permit you to involve Miss Young in any of your drunken shenanigans."

Johnny tried to punch the schoolteacher again. He missed.

"Hear now. I'm telling you to quit."

Johnny called Foster an exceeding ugly name.

The schoolmaster bristled at that. His eyes narrowed and his nostrils flared and he drew himself upright with fists formed and his skinny arms stuck out in front of him in a pose like you saw in woodcuts depicting pugilists engaging in prizefights. Johnny thought Foster looked silly as hell. He said so. And tried again to poke the schoolmaster in the nose.

Johnny felt a sort of dull sting on his face, and his eyes began to water. Had that damn Foster up and hit him one? Johnny didn't think so. He hadn't seen the schoolteacher move his hands.

Johnny tried another punch. This time he did see it. Damned old Foster hit him, sure enough. The punch snapped Johnny's head back, and a moment later he felt something warm and wet on his neck and the front of his shirt.

He was sort of dimly aware that Sarah was crying and her girlfriends were screaming and a bunch of the men and older boys were pushing every which way as some of them tried to stop the fight and others tried to get close enough to see.

Johnny saw a blur of movement and

heard the sounds of bony fists thumping into his jaw and cheeks.

It was funny, but he couldn't feel Foster's blows. He could sort of see them and he could dang sure hear them. But he couldn't hardly feel a thing.

He reeled backward, managed to right himself, and stumbled forward, intending to take a really good cut and knock that damn Foster's lights out.

Except Johnny was kneeling in the straw now, the straw he and the guys spread just that afternoon, and all he could see of damn Foster was the bastard's knees.

Johnny felt pretty lousy actually. Sick. He was gonna . . .

Johnny puked all over Ed Foster's pretty yellow spats.

Johnny didn't remember anything much after that. A glimpse of faces seen upside down. A snatch of sound or two. Feeling cold. Sensing motion around him. Like he was bumping around in the back of a dang wagon. Then even those bits and pieces went away, and he didn't know anything more.

47

"You sure made yourself plain last night."

"Yep. Made a fool of yourself too, I'd say."

"But then who woulda thought a skinny schoolteacher from Pittsburgh could put such a whipping on you."

The other voice cackled, and Johnny heard the slap of a hand against a knee. The crack of skin on cloth sounded like a can of gunpowder blowing up. He winced.

"Yeah, he's awake."

"If I was him I'd want to sleep this whole day away."

"Day? I wouldn't wanta wake up for a couple weeks anyway. Maybe longer."

Johnny lifted one eyelid and squinted against the light that streamed through the window.

"Water. Gimme some water, will you?"

Andy and Pipper seemed to think that was funny, damn them. They grinned. But

Pipper did go out and poured a dipper of water into a cup and carried it in to him.

Johnny sat up, his head pounding and his tongue feeling like it was caked thick with dried manure, and drank, the water sluicing at least some of the fur and nastiness out of his mouth.

"What're you two doing here?"

"We spent the night here. Drove you home last night after you made a complete fool o' yourself. It was late so your folks said we should bed down here for the rest of the night."

"Where . . . ?"

"They went off to church this morning. We thought we'd stay and see if you woke up."

"I wouldn't of if I'd been you," Andy said.

"I wisht I hadn't. I hurt all over."

"If you feel as bad on the inside as you look on the outside, then you're feeling mighty low, now that's a fact."

Johnny felt of his face. He didn't know what it looked like — probably was better off not knowing — but it sure as shooting was tender. He felt some hard ridges that were probably newly forming scabs, and it was hard to breathe thanks to the lumpy blood clots that caked the inside of his nose. "Jesus," he moaned.

"Too late. You shoulda got him to help you last night when you needed it."

"I need it now too. That damn schoolteacher did this to me?"

"Oh, did he ever."

"I didn't do nothing to him," Johnny complained.

Which got a laugh out of the fellows.

"You really don't remember?"

"Remember what?"

"Remember that you punched him first for openers. Hit him a pretty good lick too. Considering it would've been a miracle for you to hit the floor with your hat."

"He shook that off easier than you might think and tagged you right back."

"Then you hit the floor. Man, that skinny fella can box. He wasn't brawling with you. He was boxing."

"Knew what he was doing too, it looked like."

"Then you puked all over him and yourself and the hem of Sarah's party dress."

"I didn't."

"Sorry, but you sure as hell did, buddy."

"An' all of that was just leading up to the good stuff."

"There's more?"

"I should hope to shout."

"You got to cussing him . . . awful bad

language to holler when there's ladies around, and of course half the ladies in the basin was there . . . cussing him terrible and saying as how he was trying to steal your girl."

"And Sarah, she got to crying and everything, and her pop hustled her out of there. Didn't even wait to get their coats. Her mom grabbed those and followed along after Sarah and her father."

"And then Mr. Perkins tried to get you to shut up and get on your feet, so you cussed him some too. Loud. Real loud."

"Right there in front of the whole town?" Johnny put in.

"Yep. Right there in front of God an' everybody."

"Oh, Jesus. You shoulda left me outside so's I would take the pneumonia and die." Johnny felt like crying. "What did my folks say when you brought me home?"

"Your mom got some water and washed you up some after me and Pipper put you to bed."

"Your dad didn't say anything, though. Not one word. Not the whole rest of the night so far as I ever heard, and he wasn't any too talkative this morning neither."

"We tried to make it as better as we could. We went out and did the choring, what of it we could find to do."

"Andy hitched the wagon for your folks to take to church."

"Your father wanted to make you get up and get dressed and go with them, but your mom wouldn't let him. She said you needed to sleep."

"No, I don't need to sleep, I reckon. I need to curl up and die."

"Cheer up. You look like you're more'n halfway there already."

"Thanks. Thank you ever so much."

"Yeah, well, it's coming on toward noon, and I'm thinking your folks will be coming home from church early today. If it's all the same to you, we won't wait around for them to get here."

"We're too young an' innocent to hear the kind o' language your pop is apt to be using, Johnny. So if you'll excuse us . . ."

Johnny dropped back onto the musty, sweaty sheets, the taste of vomit lingering in his mouth along with the smell of blood in his nose.

Lordy, bad as it was, neither one of them had mentioned when he reached out and accidentally grabbed Sarah's breast.

Oh, Lordy. They really should have left him out to die last night.

He heard boots on the floor and the

door slam shut, and he was alone in the house.

Lordy, oh, Lordy, Johnny moaned piteously, feeling low and put upon and conveniently ignoring the fact that his troubles were of his own making.

But then he didn't really have to dwell too much on that. His father was sure to remind him of it.

48

His father said . . . nothing. Not a word. Johnny forced himself out of bed that afternoon and went out to do the evening chores. His father just sat in the kitchen drinking coffee and smoking his pipe, speaking very little even to Johnny's mom. And saying nothing, nothing at all, to Johnny.

The silent treatment continued until Tuesday evening, when his father finally looked him in the face — which was still bruised in rainbow hues of red and purple and dotted with scabs here and there — and spoke.

"Outside."

"Yes, sir." Johnny sighed and marched dutifully out into the yard, which was covered with dirty, boot-churned snow. He shivered, but did not bother to button his coat. After all, he expected to be taking it off again right away so it wouldn't impede his father's apple-wood switch.

The switch stood in a corner of the barn where they kept saddles and harness and suchlike. It was long and whippy and hurt like hell when it was applied. As Johnny knew all too well. He could remember that switch for as long as . . . well, for as long as he could remember just about anything.

When Johnny was just a button and the family still lived back in Kansas, they'd had some apple trees. Every spring his father would prune away the suckers that sprouted on the bearing branches. The whipping switch was one of those long, limber suckers that his father trimmed smooth and then wrapped with twine at the thick end so as to make a handle. He'd used that same switch on Johnny's back, legs, and butt for all that time, moving it right along with them when they came to Montana Territory.

Johnny hated that damn switch. Still did, even though it had been two, three years or maybe longer since he'd felt the cut of it across his backside. Many a time he'd wanted to break it in two and have the pleasure of burning the thing, but it wasn't his place to do that, which would probably just make his father furious and cause all manner of problems.

Now Johnny was wishing he'd gone ahead and got rid of the switch when he'd had the chance.

Johnny trudged into the barn and, resigned, found the switch and handed it to his father.

"What's this?"

"The . . . you know."

"I'll be damned. I didn't know we still had this old thing."

He didn't *know?* His father didn't even realize they still had the switch that Johnny so loathed and, truth be, feared? Good God!

Lewis Ackerman stood the switch back in the corner where it had been all this time and turned to face his rather battered son.

"Boy, it's about time you and me have a talk about all the ignorant, damn-fool things you went and did last Saturday night."

"Yes, sir."

"We won't go into what-all those things were. You know what you did."

Which was a wildly over-optimistic assumption, the truth being that Johnny had very little recollection of what those things were. And would have known even less if it hadn't been for the fellows telling him some of it on Sunday.

Of course, that lack of knowledge probably should be considered an act of great mercy.

"As it happens," his father was saying, "your mother and I know all about it too. You were the principal subject of conversation after services on Sunday. Only to be expected, of course. After all, stupidity that publicly spectacular doesn't come along just every Saturday night."

"No, sir." Johnny felt a thickness in his throat and a heaviness in his chest. Everyone knew. He understood that they would. Of course he did. But to be told now how it was all dragged out and discussed in front of his mother . . . He'd done more than act like an idiot. He'd gone and hurt his mother too. That made him feel lower than ever.

"I have been thinking about what I should say to you, John. Or do to you."

"Whatever it is, I reckon I deserve it."

"Yes, you most certainly do. Now first, son . . ."

Johnny had no appetite at supper that evening. None. And not much of an opinion of himself either.

Sarah wouldn't have any sort of opinion of him either. None that was good anyway.

He'd really gone and done it, damn him.

49

"Pop, tomorrow I need to check those three water holes on the upper creek, but after I'm done with that I think I'm gonna go into town."

It had been three weeks since Johnny showed his face in Redhorse Butte. He hadn't ridden into town in that time nor gone to church nor so much as ridden over to visit with Pipper or with Andy. He'd spent his time working or sulking in the curtained-off cubicle that held his bed. He'd brooded. And he'd healed. And now it was time to start putting the incident behind him.

As soon as he took care of one or two things, that is. He reached for the bowl of mashed potatoes and the gravy boat beside it.

"Johnny, dear, just be careful you don't . . ."

"It's all right, Stella," his father said.

221

"He's old enough to make a jackass of himself. Now we'll find out if he's strong enough to live it down as well."

Johnny nodded. "I'll head to town then once I get done riding the creek bank."

"What about your dinner tomorrow, dear?"

"I'll carry a lunch with me, Mama. If I need anything more than that I can get something in town."

"Do you have any money?"

"No, sir."

Without speaking, Johnny's father went to the tin box where they kept their cash. He took out a pair of silver cartwheels and handed them to Johnny.

It was something of a test, Johnny suspected. That was enough to buy a quart of trade whiskey if that's what he chose to do.

"Thank you." Johnny didn't comment on the amount, nor did his father. His mother probably did not make the connection.

"I won't short the water holes," he promised.

"Never thought you would, son. Ma, how's about giving me another helping of those field peas, will you, and maybe a little more of the coffee too."

50

Johnny left the road a couple miles from town and swung out to the north so he could come in behind the outlying buildings instead of riding down the main street. His expression was grim. But then so was his purpose.

A glance toward the sun, riding so low in the sky it was turning red, showed him it was very late in the afternoon. That should be about right, he figured.

He tied his horse to the teeter-totter behind the schoolhouse, removed his coat and draped it over his saddle, then hung his hat on the saddle horn. He kept his gloves on, however.

The damn schoolmaster was still there. Johnny found him pushing a wet mop to clean up the small, muddy footprints his pupils left behind.

Foster looked up when Johnny came in. He nodded. "I'm pleased to see you're all right, Ackerman, but shouldn't you be wearing a coat in weather like this?"

"I'll worry about my own welfare, thank you."

Foster shrugged and set his mop aside. "Is there something I can do for you, Ackerman? I don't want to be late for supper. Mrs. Marrick is proud of the table she sets, and I wouldn't want to disappoint her."

"You know what I want, schoolteacher."

"Do I?"

"Don't give me any of that Mr. Innocence crap. Last time I saw you I was drunk. You took advantage of me so's you could look good in front of my girl. The thing is, today I ain't drunk."

"Ackerman, you made a fool of yourself once at that dance. Don't compound the error by doing it again."

"I can whip you, Foster."

"Frankly I doubt that. But even if you are right, what would that prove? Beating another person does not make you better than he. Nor smarter. It certainly doesn't make you right. So what is your point in being here?"

"My point is that you took advantage of a drunk so's you could play the big man.

Well, you're nothing but a city-raised weakling, and I intend to prove it right here an' now."

"I have no quarrel with you, Ackerman, and I have no intention to fight with you. There is no reason for it."

"How about this as a reason." Johnny lashed out with his right fist. The blow smacked hard on the schoolteacher's left cheek, snapping his head back and rocking him, but not putting him down as Johnny had intended.

Foster stepped back. He pressed the back of his hand to the flushed red blotch on his cheek, but he neither retreated into the schoolhouse nor tried to attack Johnny. He just stood there.

"I do not want to fight with you, Ackerman. It will serve no purpose."

"You're right. Won't serve any purpose at all, for I intend to whip your ass whether you fight back or not. It don't make any difference to me either way."

Johnny stepped forward and swung at Foster again.

This time, though, the schoolmaster swayed to the side just enough to slip Johnny's punch. Johnny's fist slashed wickedly — but harmlessly — past his face.

Foster's left hand flashed, and Johnny

felt the sting of a slap on his own cheek.

A *slap!* Like as if he were a little kid being disciplined for telling a fib.

Weeks of pent-up rage, poorly contained ever since that night at the dance, boiled up inside Johnny's chest and sent a red haze of anger through him that clouded both his vision and his judgment.

He launched himself at the schoolteacher, intending to batter, to beat down into the ground, to utterly destroy.

Foster looked almost sad as he slid quickly to one side and let Johnny's own momentum carry him past.

Johnny felt another sting, a hard one this time, on his temple.

He stumbled and went to his knees on the damp, just-mopped floor.

"Damn you!"

"Get control of yourself, Ackerman. I was champion pugilist at Bilrovic Normal School. I can do this all day and you won't touch me. Now calm down and . . ."

Foster sidestepped again as Johnny rushed him. This time the schoolmaster did not even hit him. Johnny lost his balance and went down anyway.

"Damn you. Damn you t' hell an' gone," Johnny cried.

"Quit it, Ackerman. You're making a

fool of yourself again. Now stop this and go home."

Close to tears, Johnny gathered himself and came upright. He balled his fists and launched himself forward.

A hint of daylight remained in the sky when Johnny left the schoolhouse and wobbled back to his horse.

It hurt to reach high enough to reclaim his hat and coat. Hurt far worse to crawl awkwardly onto his saddle. Hurt most of all to realize that he'd been bested. Badly. Beaten by a useless damn fancy boy.

He felt like crying as he turned his horse's head toward home.

51

Johnny heard the hoofbeats of an approaching horse. He cocked his head and listened, then amended that to the approach of at least two horses as they came closer and he could hear them better. With a reluctant sigh he stood and went to the small window set into the front wall.

It was Sunday morning, and his folks had gone to church. They'd wanted him to go with them, but stopped short of making an issue of it. Johnny was in no humor to go out in public again. He had not told his parents about being whipped by Ed Foster for the second time, and oddly enough, last Sunday they had not said anything to him about the gossip that must surely be going around town. Again.

Now Pipper and Andy were skipping church services too and coming to visit. Johnny was not at all sure he wanted to face them, but he had no choice about it. They were already here.

His friends dismounted and tied their horses to the corral rails, then ambled across the yard to the house.

It was a gorgeous day, the sun bright and warm enough that the air temperature seemed hardly to matter, and both of them had their coats unbuttoned. The recent snowfall was almost completely melted now, and the ground was bare except on the shaded north sides of buildings, slopes, or what have you. The only thing ugly about the day was Johnny's mood.

"Hey, buddy," Andy said, letting himself in without knocking. "How're you doing?"

"I'm okay."

"You sure? It's near two months since the dance, and nobody's seen hide nor hair of you since. So how come you're hiding out here instead of coming in and having some fun with us now an' then?"

Johnny wondered why they hadn't mentioned his humiliation in that second fight with the schoolmaster, but all he said was, "D'you want some coffee?"

"Sure."

"That sounds good, thanks."

Johnny took down some enamelware mugs from the cupboard he and his father had built — or more accurately from the cupboard his father had constructed despite Johnny's little-boy attempts to help — and poured from the pot that was left over from breakfast.

Pipper took a flat pint bottle out of his coat pocket and tipped some whiskey into his cup and Andy's. Johnny put a hand over his cup, though, to stop Pipper from adding any "sweetener" to it.

"What's the matter? You don't drink no more?"

Johnny shook his head. Pipper shrugged and pressed the cork back into the neck of the bottle.

"Look, man, are you done sitting out here hiding out from everybody?"

"I don't know. I . . . just don't know yet."

"Well, you'd best get done with it. It ain't the same without you around, Johnny. We all of us miss you. And there's no need for you to stay out here by yourself, y'know."

"You were drunk that night, buddy. Everybody understands that. Nobody's holding anything against you."

"Sarah is," Johnny said.

"No, she isn't."

"Oh, hell, she's bound to be. I poked her right in the tit. Did you know that? It was by accident, but I did it. And then I puked on her dress. And worst of all, I got showed up by that damned schoolteacher."

"Johnny, I'm telling you, everybody understands. You had a little too much to drink, that's all. It's no big deal. You know?"

"I just can't go and face Sarah again, fellas. I can't even imagine what she must be thinking about me now. I just can't."

"You want proof that she don't feel like you think she does?"

"What d'you mean by proof, huh?"

Andy grinned and reached inside his coat. He brought out a tiny envelope and handed it over. "John Ackerman" was written on the front in bold, ornately curly handwriting.

"What the . . . ?"

"It's an invitation, man."

"To Sarah's birthday party. She'll be sweet sixteen, you know."

"And never been kissed." Pipper grinned knowingly. "Or so the saying claims anyway."

"She found us at Archer's yesterday and asked us special to bring this out to you. We got invitations too, of course. I guess pretty much all the kids did. But she made a point of wanting you there, man."

"It'd be a big insult if you refuse to go after . . . you know."

Johnny's heart began to race. Sarah wanted him to come to her party? Damn. And after Foster whipped him twice?

He wondered if the schoolteacher hadn't bragged about that to anybody. Surely Pipper and Andy would be ragging on him about it if they knew. And if Foster mentioned it to anybody in the whole town, the word would've flown through the whole dang basin in less than a day. Andy and Pipper would be sure to have heard.

But nobody seemed to know about that, and Sarah apparently was willing to excuse his drunken lapse at the Christmas dance.

Maybe . . .

"You'll come?" Andy asked. "It's to be next Saturday afternoon. It ought to be fun."

"Say you'll come, Johnny," Pipper urged.

Johnny smiled. "What the hell. Yeah. You can tell Sarah I'll be coming to her party."

He still had a chance with Sarah. That was the thing. He still had a chance. Hot damn!

52

Oh, Johnny did look fine. Starched and buttoned, brushed and slicked down. He even went in early enough to stop at Perkins's barbershop and get himself a shave and a dash of bay rum behind his ears and never mind that it was not strictly necessary for him to shave, his beard being no more than a little pale hair that his pop claimed a cat could lick off easier than scrape it away with a razor. To which Johnny's every-time response was, "We don't have a dang cat or maybe I'd try it your way."

Mr. Perkins didn't make any comments, thank goodness. Of course he had thirteen cents cash money at stake in the matter, and Johnny's father did not.

The party was at Sarah's house, where somebody had gone to a lot of trouble making everything festive and just so.

There were crepe streamers of every color imaginable — well, if your imagination was limited to yellow, pink, white, and green — strung from the walls so that everything crisscrossed in the middle, and at that point where the streamers came together there was a bouquet of ribbons and artificial flowers big enough that the girls must have denuded every Sunday hat in the neighborhood to put it together.

All the furniture in the parlor and the dining room too had been pushed back against the walls so there was room for everyone to crowd in.

The dining table was covered with an embroidered linen tablecloth that was whiter than any winter snow, and there was a hodgepodge of glasses and cups and mugs — pretty near anything that would hold liquid — set around a punch bowl big enough to wash a week of clothes in.

The punch was a mixture of cold tea and fruit juices. There were slices of fresh orange floating in it along with a chunk of ice big as a muskmelon.

There were cookies and slices of fruitcake and chewy boiled cookies and salted nuts and some little mincemeat tarts.

Oh, it was grand, and everyone stood around looking subdued and formal in their extra-best clothes.

Johnny never in his life saw such a fine soiree.

But then a young lady doesn't get to turn sixteen just every old day. After all, that was an occasion that marked her passage from being a girl to being a marriageable young woman.

Marriageable. Oh, Lordy! Sarah was come of age. The mere thought of that put Johnny in an amorous mood, and he had to turn around and face away from everybody for a minute there until he got control of the problem.

Sarah was standing in the parlor close to the vestibule — he did remember that vestibule, he surely did — where she could greet everybody as they came in. Her expression when she first saw Johnny was sweet and perfectly normal, like she really didn't hold any grudges against him for that horrible mess at the dance. And like she didn't know about the other time either.

Johnny looked around right off, but he didn't see Foster. The schoolteacher was sure to be there, though, and Johnny wasn't sure how he ought to act when that happened.

He could worry about that later, though.

For the time being he stepped up before

Sarah and dug a package out of his coat pocket. It was only brown butcher paper tied with a scrap of well-used ribbon, but it was the best he had to offer.

He shoved it toward Sarah and explained, "I worked evenings on it all week. I hope you like it."

"You made it? Just for me?"

He bobbed his head, and Sarah smiled until her dimples showed. "I know I'll like it," she said in that sweet, soft voice.

Later on, when Ed Foster did walk in, there turned out to be no trouble, no problems at all. The schoolmaster smiled to the room full of folks in general, but the only one he singled out was Sarah.

He too had a present for the birthday girl, and Johnny managed to slip in close enough that he could see what it was. It was a book, small and squat with leather binding and the title in gold leaf. Something about *Collected Poems*. Johnny didn't bother looking to see whose poems. He probably wouldn't have known who it was if he did see. And certainly wouldn't care.

Sarah made noises like she just loved it. But then she was doing that every time anybody handed her a birthday present.

For a moment Johnny wondered if

maybe he should have gone to Archer's and bought something. Like a book of poems, for instance.

But dang it, he'd spent hours and hours making that horsehair fob for her. In four different colors of hair, for which he'd had to ride over to the LYK to get some tail hair as the Ackermans only had three colors from their own animals.

And anyway, every kid in town knew every item Mr. Archer had in his place for sale and what it cost.

It was better, Johnny decided, to give something that was a part of himself instead of some stupid book of poetry.

All in all, it turned out to be one hell of a fine birthday party. And not one soul so much as mentioned the last time he'd been around folks.

53

Johnny waited impatiently for the church service to end and Mr. Tolliver to give the benediction.

As soon as it was ended and everyone had started into the aisles, the women turning the pews into makeshift tables for lunch and the men going out front to smoke and talk while the kids and youngsters brought in the heavily laden lunch baskets, he pushed through the crowd and hurried outside.

Instead of going to their wagon right off to fetch in the lunch his mom had been packing roughly since the break of day, Johnny ran around back so he would be there when the choir came out.

Sarah was next to last through the door, trailed by Ed Foster, who pretended not to notice that Johnny was there.

"Sarah, could I speak with you for a moment?"

"Of course."

Johnny stood there looking pointedly at Foster until the schoolmaster got the message and excused himself. He looked like he didn't particularly want to, but he went off alone toward the front of the church. Every week Mrs. Marrick packed enough lunch for their boarder too.

Johnny waited until Foster was far enough away to not overhear, then said, "I was noticing during church that you look pale. I think you might be coming down with something. A stomach ache maybe?"

"Johnny, I feel perfectly fine."

"No, I'm pretty sure that you don't." He was grinning shyly. And hopefully. He'd lain awake thinking about this half the night last night. Or at least it felt like a long time. "I really think you have a stomach ache, Sarah. Eating all that heavy stuff at the potluck today would make it worse. I'm certain of that."

"John Ackerman, what *are* you up to?"

"What I was kinda thinking, see, is that if you aren't feeling too well, I could drive you home in our wagon. You know. So your folks can stay here to eat an' hear the second part of the service. I know what store they set on Mr. Tolliver's preaching. I wouldn't want them to miss any of it. So what I was thinking is that I could drive you to town an' then come back for my folks. Get here in time to pick them up after church."

"And is it only driving that you have in mind, pray tell?"

Johnny laughed. He would have kissed her right there and then, this grown-up and entirely marriageable young woman, except of course they were standing right outside the church building and anybody might look outside and see.

"You are a wicked, wicked person, John. Wicked."

"But, um, are you feeling sick now?"

"Now that you mention it, I think I do feel a little queasy."

"Go tell your folks, hear? I'll go in an' tell mine, then get the wagon and meet you around front."

Sarah giggled and with a light, springing step ran toward the front doors. Just short of the corner of the building, though, she remembered to slow down and adopt a solemn and pain-wracked expression, holding her stomach and walking just the least bit bent over.

She was, after all, feeling very sick to her stomach.

54

"We're here."

"Yes. Yes, I see that we are."

They were stopped in front of the Youngs' house, and Johnny was nervous. He jumped down from the wagon and came around to Sarah's side so he could help her to the ground. He offered his arm and escorted her to the door.

"I, uh . . ."

"Come inside, Johnny. Here. You can help me off with my cloak. Hang it over there, please." She smiled. "Thank you."

After a moment Sarah said, "Aren't you going to take off your coat? I mean . . . you do intend to sit with me awhile, don't you?" The smile returned. "And talk? Or something?"

The house felt large and empty with no one else there but the two of them. It had a different feel to it now than when the whole family was inside.

There was nothing to stop him from . . .

"Shall we use the settee?" Sarah suggested before he finished the exciting but oh-so-daring thought.

"Yeah. Sure."

He dropped his coat beside the vestibule entrance and followed her to the settee. Sarah settled gracefully onto the middle, leaving him no option but to sit very close to her.

Johnny's palms were damp and there was a catch in his throat when he sat. He was acutely conscious of Sarah's warmth. And her beauty. He wanted to grab her. Hug her. Kiss her. He wanted to do . . . things . . . with her. Things he could scarcely imagine doing in real life. Things he barely understood if the truth of it were known.

"I, uh . . ."

"Johnny."

"Yes?"

"Aren't you going to kiss me?"

With a barely muffled moan, he lifted his arm. Pulled her to him.

His mouth found hers. She was eager. Accepting. Her tongue fluttered and probed, and Johnny felt weak. His breath quickened, and he held her fiercely close.

They fell into the corner of the settee,

Johnny half-reclining there, Sarah lying partially on top of him.

Her body was warm and small and mobile as she writhed slightly.

Johnny's reaction was powerful, unstoppable, and this time Sarah had to be aware of it.

They kissed until Johnny's lips became sore and he began to pant with desire for this wonderful, beautiful, adorable girl who was his very own.

Without consciously willing it, his hand found the proud, firm swell of her breast. He cupped her flesh. Lightly squeezed.

He really expected her to draw back and slap him. She did not. Sarah was breathing heavily too. Her body was moving.

It was obvious even in his inexperience that she too was aroused. He hadn't known that girls had such physical reactions. Hadn't known that girls could experience the same sort of desire that boys do. It was a revelation to him but one he would examine later.

He touched her breast, then became all the bolder and fumbled to open the buttons at the top of her dress.

Again he truly expected Sarah to object. She did pull a few inches back. Instead of getting up from the settee, she pushed his hand down off her breast, getting it out of the way so she could undo the buttons herself.

"Oh, God," he groaned as his hand found the silken warmth of her flesh. He had never touched anything so taut and firm yet at the same time soft.

There were hard little bumps on the tip ends of her breasts. He didn't know what those were, but . . . Sarah tugged on the back of his head and he was able to see, to touch, to taste these marvelous little pink protrusions.

"Jesus," he whispered.

"Shhh. Hush now."

Sarah shifted position, and — incredibly — he felt her touch. *Her* touch. On him. Dear God!

Her hand slid inside the waistband of his Sunday trousers. And lower.

He cried out and . . . Oh, Lordy. Oh, damn.

Sarah giggled. "It's messy, isn't it."

Johnny felt the heat of a first-class blush light up his cheeks. Sheepishly he said, "Yeah, I guess 'tis."

Sarah kissed him. A quick peck on the lips this time. "It's all right. I understand. I think."

Lordy, he hoped so.

She withdrew her hand from inside his trousers and said, "Excuse me, please. I think I'd better go wash now."

"Sure. Sure thing."

"Johnny, I think . . . I really think we should stop now. Don't you agree?"

Hell, no, he didn't agree. "Yes, I think you're right."

She stood up, holding her hand well away from her dress, and headed toward the kitchen.

"Sarah."

"Yes?"

"I love you."

Her smile was dear and her dimples adorable. "You're sweet, Johnny. Thank you."

Then she was gone.

Later, a very little while later, Johnny headed for home. He was almost there before he remembered that he was supposed to go back to the church now and pick up his parents.

55

The thought of marriage was a daunting thing. Johnny hadn't yet proven himself in the world. He had no firm prospects, not even any real plans. Except marriage. Oh, he did plan and hope and dream when it came to the marriage part. And the intimacy between a husband and his wife. Especially when it came to that intimacy.

Even so, in his more honest moments, he realized that he had damned good reason to be nervous.

Marriage is a huge weight of responsibility. Scary. He would be solely responsible not only for himself but for Sarah too.

If it were only his own well-being at stake, he wouldn't worry at all. He could manage. Find a job. Ride the grub line if necessary and bum a meal off whatever ranches he came to and sleep wherever darkness overtook him. Heck, that would even be kind of romantic and adventuresome.

But a fellow couldn't do that if he had a wife to take care of too.

And Sarah, she was a gentle girl with no experience of hardship. Besides, she deserved the best that life has to offer. She deserved nice clothes and a full larder and a home she could be proud of. A husband she could be proud of too.

When he thought about things like that, Johnny became apprehensive and very nearly sad.

Yet how could he be sad when he had Sarah Young, soon to be Sarah Young Ackerman, for his own?

He would have to . . . he wasn't sure what he would have to do. His half-formed idea about taking up land and starting a small ranch of his own was an unrealistic dream now. Something like that takes time. And money. The land was one thing. The least of things really.

Heck, there was more than enough land free for the taking. His dad had explained how that worked. You filed on the quarter section that was allowed, and you located that so it controlled water. Whoever controls the water controls whatever grass is around it. So a quarter section owned could mean half-a-dozen whole sections under exclusive use simply because no one else's cattle could have access to that water.

Then you filed for an additional piece that you pledged to reforest. The government allowed that, and if you planted a few twigs that was enough to satisfy the rule. And of course you located that so it controlled some water too.

And then you got your wife to do the same thing in her own name.

When all was said and done, you could end up either owning or controlling a dozen sections or more of grazing land. And that was enough to carry a nice-sized herd.

Except . . . you had to have a herd in order for that land to mean anything.

Johnny and Sarah could go right out and take up the land if they liked. Right now, or just as quick as they got married.

But he had nothing to put on the land. No money for timber to build a house. No money even for a plow to cut sod and build a house out of that. No money for tools or for breeding stock or for . . . anything.

What it all came down to was that if they got married now — and they pretty much had to get married now after what they'd done on Sunday afternoon — ranching just wasn't going to be possible.

Johnny would have to get a job, that was all. Doing something. It didn't matter what. He was willing to turn his hand to just about anything that would make a living for them. He was strong. He was willing. He might not have much in the way of skills, but he would do any sort of labor that would make them a living.

There wasn't anything around Redhorse Butte, of course. They would have to move to a city someplace. Anyplace where there was work, was the way he saw it.

Johnny had scant experience with cities. Only one really, and that was Cheyenne when he was a kid and the family moved up from Kansas. They just passed through, not even stopping there for a night, and he did not remember much of anything about it.

Except that his mom bought him a poke of horehound candies at a store close to the railroad depot in Cheyenne. There was an Indian in the store and that scared him. He remembered that well enough. But except for that . . .

Well, they would just have to go to a city, that was all. They could go to whatever one Sarah wanted. And Johnny would find work there, and they would rent a little house and it would be wonderful. Just wonderful.

Johnny sighed. There was so much they needed to talk about, so much they needed to work out between them.

But the really important stuff, that was already decided.

He grinned and wiggled his fingers and wrinkled his nose.

His backside was numb from being wet and cold, and he had a drip — maybe frozen by now — under his nose that he couldn't wipe off.

But his hand was warm. That was certainly so, for it was a foot and a half deep inside this dang heifer what was having trouble with a calf that needed to be turned the right way to so it could be birthed, and why in the *hell* had the calving got started now when Johnny needed to get away to town so he could see Sarah and get some things settled?

Damn cows had no consideration or they would've waited a little before they started this nonsense.

Johnny heard his father's footsteps crunching through last year's dry, brittle grass. He looked up and grinned.

"Got that one under control, son?"

"Yes, sir, I think so."

"All right then. I'm going to check the other side of the hill there and see if there's any more in labor. I think we've about got all of them right close around here." His father smiled. "Until tonight or tomorrow. I've noticed a couple others with their teats waxing up and their bags getting full. That's most generally the sign they're about due."

"Yes, sir." Johnny sighed.

"Something wrong?"

"No, I was just . . . I was just wanting a little time. To ride into town for a few hours. You know?"

"Is there something in particular you need to do?"

Johnny didn't answer. But the heat rushed into his cheeks.

"Oh, I see. In that case perhaps you'd best not answer that question," his dad said.

Johnny gave his father a grateful look. Then became serious again and groped a little deeper inside the wet heat of the cow. "I think . . . there! I got it."

There was a moist plop as he pulled his hand free and rolled away from the rather messy back end of the animal. Seconds later the small, pink, pointy front hoofs of a newly borning calf made their appearance, and a soft nose soon after.

Lewis Ackerman helped the calf out the last little way, and then they turned the job over to the mama cow.

"You did good," his father said.

"You talking to me?" Johnny asked. "Or that heifer?"

"Stick with me here a little longer, son, until the birthing slacks off. Then I'll give you a little something for a wage and you can go in and have yourself some fun."

"All right, Pop. Thanks."

Johnny used a piece of stiff, blood-crusted rag to wipe down his arm just a little, then he and his father headed for their horses. There were bound to be more cattle in need of assistance with their calving.

56

Johnny tied his horse outside the Young home and mounted the front porch. He was excited. What he thought they should do — and he had given it a great deal of thought over the past week and a half of nonstop calving — was for Sarah to stay here in Redhorse Butte while he went down to Cheyenne . . . or further if need be . . . to find a job and a place to rent.

That should take, oh, call it a month. Maybe two. Two months would be perfect actually. That would give Sarah time enough to finish school and get her diploma as a high school graduate.

Naturally she wouldn't need to take the teaching examination over the summer. A housewife has more than enough work to do without trying to work outside the home. And anyway, no school board would hire a married woman to teach.

Teachers are supposed to be pure.

Women teachers anyway. Johnny would've been willing to wager that that sonuvabitch Ed Foster hadn't a pure bone nor a pure thought anywhere in him.

Not that that was of interest to him. Not really. It would've been nice to whip the damn schoolmaster and get that back on him. But it wasn't important. Compared with Sarah, there wasn't much of anything he would consider important. Not down-deep, really and truly important.

Ed Foster could go hang for all he cared. Johnny had the true prize and that was what counted.

He tapped on the door and took his hat off when Mrs. Young answered his knock. "Ma'am," he said, feeling kind of shy considering what-all happened the last time he was in this house, "I was hoping I might have a word with Sarah this afternoon."

They wouldn't be able to take up where they left off the other time, not with her mother home, but that was all right. He could wait.

God, he loved her. He would wade through a sea of fire and wait forever so long as he knew Sarah would be waiting on the other side of pain and sorrow.

"Hello, dear," Mrs. Young said. She was wearing a flour-smeared apron and had a dish towel in her hands. "Sarah is still at the school studying for that teaching examination. My, but there must be a lot she has to learn."

"Yes, ma'am."

"I'll tell you what, Johnny. When you see her, tell her I'd like for her to come home soon." The woman smiled. "Why don't you walk her home, then the two of you can come inside and have a snack. I'm baking a cobbler."

"You make the finest cobbler I've ever had, ma'am. That'd be real nice."

"Why, thank you, dear. That's sweet of you to say so, especially after I've tasted your mother's cobblers. Mine can't hold a candle to hers."

Johnny didn't offer any argument, if only because it was true. His mom's cobblers really were better. But he did not want to come right out and say so. "Thank you, ma'am. I'll have her home directly." He bobbed his head and put his hat back on and went out to the street and on past where his horse was tied. There was no point in riding over to the schoolhouse if he was just going to turn right around and walk Sarah home again.

It wasn't all that cold an afternoon, but for some reason Johnny felt a chill on the back of his neck.

57

Johnny frowned. He wasn't so much worried as he was puzzled. Mrs. Young said Sarah was here. And he thought he heard voices coming from inside the schoolhouse. But the front door was locked.

Hell, Johnny hadn't even known the building had a lock. It wasn't like there was any reason to lock a nearly empty place like the school. Folks didn't even bother locking their homes around here.

Well, maybe Mr. Archer and some of the merchants locked their stores. He didn't actually know about that.

But the school?

He walked around to the side. The windows were open, which probably accounted for him being able to hear. Around beside the building he could hear better. It was . . .

Johnny went pale.

He crouched down low and crept underneath the window toward the back, toward where the schoolmaster's desk was.

He raised up and peered inside.

Time, sound, thought . . . the whole damned world came to a sudden halt.

Sarah was at the school, all right. So was that son of a puling bitch Ed Foster.

Sarah was laid back over top of the teacher's desk.

The front of her dress was opened, and her skirt was pushed up waist-high. Foster was licking and suckling on her left titty. And his hand. Oh, Jesus, he'd pulled her drawers down to her knees and he was feeling of her. Down there.

Oh, God, it was awful.

Johnny cried out. He couldn't help himself. He let out an anguished wail. The terrible cry was ripped out of his belly and went soaring up to heaven carrying all the world's hurt in the sound of it.

God, no!

Sarah sat bolt upright. Foster took his hand out from under Sarah's skirt and sat back in the spring-loaded swivel chair that the people of Redhorse Butte provided for his comfort.

Neither one of them looked the least bit ashamed, but Sarah looked angry.

"You filthy little spy!"

"I . . . Jesus, Sarah, I . . ."

"You were spying on me. Admit it. You were spying."

"No, I . . . Sarah, how could you do something like this? I thought . . . I thought we was gonna get married. I thought we was engaged. I thought you loved me. God knows, I love you."

"Johnny, you silly, stupid damn hayseed. Do you really think I want to spend the rest of my life raising babies and washing horse shit off your pants? You're a nice-looking boy, Johnny, but you're a play-thing, that's all. So is Eddie here, but he doesn't mind. At least Eddie is helping me get the hell out of this stupid little town.

"I'm going to Denver, Johnny. Or Kansas City even. Chicago. Paris or London. Why not? I can go and do anything I like, and what I like has nothing to do with you or your dreary kind. Now get out of here will you, please, and let us get back to what we were doing."

Sarah paused and gave him a wickedly haughty look. "Or would you like me to tell everyone that I caught you peeping. How would you like that, Johnny? Do you want me to tell everybody you're a Peeping Tom? That would be nice, wouldn't it, after the Christmas dance.

Now get out of here. Leave me alone."

"I really think you should go, Ackerman," Foster sneered. "Or would you like me to give you another boxing lesson, eh?"

Johnny reeled backward in shock, then stumbled blindly away.

He was . . . Sarah . . . she . . . and Foster . . . like that . . . ugly.

He began to cry.

58

"Say there, Johnny. Are you all right? Forgive me for saying so, but you don't look well this afternoon."

Johnny brushed past Mr. Archer without speaking and ran to the rack behind the counter where the storekeeper kept the few firearms he stocked.

Johnny grabbed for the big Winchester '76 that he'd always admired. It was a beautiful thing, the Montana Bear Rifle. Powerful.

The boxes of cartridges had been sitting inside Mr. Archer's display case since he'd first gotten the rifles in. The pasteboard containers were sun-faded and flyspecked after all this time, while the popular shotshell boxes were clean and new.

Johnny took a box of cartridges out and tore it open on the countertop.

"What's wrong, son? Did your horse break its leg or something? I'm sorry,

Johnny. I know that can be an awful thing. But don't you want to use something a little less, shall we say, drastic to shoot him with? I have a pistol here I could loan you. Why don't you . . . ?"

Still without speaking to the friendly merchant Johnny tumbled a handful of the squat, heavy .45–60 cartridges into his pocket, took some more in his fist, and trotted outside, shoving the blunt rounds into the rifle's magazine as he went.

He ran across the street and through an alley behind the line of Redhorse Butte's businesses.

When the Winchester was fully loaded, he opened his hand and let all the remaining cartridges fall to the ground.

This time Johnny did not bother trying the locked schoolhouse door.

He paused for a moment, his breathing labored, to steady himself. Then he lifted his boot high and lasted out, striking with the heel beside the lock plate.

The latch broke and part of the door frame shattered beside it. The door flew open with a crash, and Johnny dashed inside.

Foster and Sarah were still there, but now they were bent over the desk pretending to study. Both were fully clothed,

Sarah's dress primly buttoned to the throat.

"Is there something you want, John?" Sarah asked in a falsely sweet voice.

"You . . ." His face twisted and he had to stop and get control of himself, fighting against an overwhelming urge to bawl and blubber. He did not want to do that. It would be embarrassing — embarrassment piled atop of embarrassment — and did *not*.

"You thought I'd bring folks, didn't you. You thought I'd try an' get you caught doing those awful things."

Sarah looked up and laughed. "Face it, Johnny. I'm out of your league."

"Just a little more practice and she will be out of mine too, Ackerman. The girl is a natural. Accept that and let her go. She will go to some lucky city, Ackerman, and end up as a whore. Do you know why? Because she likes it. That is the very best kind, you see. Believe me, I know." Foster gave him another of those snotty looks.

"You can both go to Hell, damn you."

"Perhaps," Foster said. "Someday."

"No, damn you. Right now!"

They may not even have noticed the Winchester he'd been carrying muzzle-down beside his right leg.

They certainly saw it when he lifted it now.

Behind him Johnny could hear the sound of running feet and shouting voices.

Mr. Archer must have seen him run into the schoolhouse instead of going to the aid of an injured horse.

The folks were coming. They would be there soon.

"Oh, Jesus God!" Johnny cried. His words were a plea and a prayer and not an epithet. "Dear Jesus, God."

He worked the stiffly new lever down and back up again, chambering a cartridge and bringing the big rifle to full cock.

"Johnny, sweetheart. Don't."

"Oh, hell, dear. If the fool wants to shoot himself, let him. But not in the head if you please, Ackerman. I'm the one who will have to clean up your mess, so do me a favor and shoot yourself in the chest, will you?" Ed Foster did not sound at all frightened.

Johnny had nothing to say to that.

59

Sam Archer was thinking he was getting just too damned old for this running and hollering stuff. He slowed his pace a little and waited for some of the others to catch up.

"What's the matter, Sam? What's wrong?"

"I think . . . Johnny Ackerman . . . in the school," Archer panted. "With a . . . rifle."

"What happened, Sam? A raccoon get loose in there or something?"

"I don't . . . think so."

Archer came to a complete stop and leaned down to rest his hands on his knees as he tried to get some air into his aching lungs. "I think . . ."

Whatever he thought or might have said was blotted out by the hard, dull roar of a large-caliber rifle being fired.

There was that gunshot. A half second's pause and then another.

"What the hell was that?" someone shouted.

Two, three, perhaps four seconds, and a third gunshot reverberated through the schoolhouse.

Several of the men dashed up the steps and through the shattered door.

"Oh, God. Oh, no!"

Others crowded inside to witness the horror of all that blood and the three bodies sprawled in the center of the slowly spreading crimson lake.

"Oh, Jesus."

Archer stayed where he was, probably the only adult male in town that late afternoon who did not push his way inside so he could see. He already suspected what was there, and he did not want to see it.

Besides, somebody needed to go find Fred Tolliver. Fred would have to be the one to tell George and Ada Young. And then Lewis and Stella.

Sam took a deep breath. He supposed he should ride along with Fred. That would be the Christian thing to do.

Archer turned and walked with a heavy step and a heavier heart to the blacksmith's shop where he hoped to God Fred would be this afternoon.

But whatever in the world would they

tell the Youngs and the Ackermans? They would have questions. There were no answers.

"Jesus!" Archer whispered aloud.

The employees of Thorndike Press hope you have enjoyed this Large Print book. All our Thorndike and Wheeler Large Print titles are designed for easy reading, and all our books are made to last. Other Thorndike Press Large Print books are available at your library, through selected bookstores, or directly from us.

For information about titles, please call:

(800) 223-1244

or visit our Web site at:

www.gale.com/thorndike
www.gale.com/wheeler

To share your comments, please write:

Publisher
Thorndike Press
295 Kennedy Memorial Drive
Waterville, ME   04901